At 15, Rory McAlister [...] to Mr Cornwallis, the w[...] [...]mall village of Wind Fell near South Shields in the north of England. His only concerns were for the well being of his family, and his overriding desire to relieve them from poverty and to marry Lily, the blacksmith's daughter.

All this was to change when, injured in the sawpit, Mr Cornwallis is confined to his bed. This happens only a few days before a planned visit to his 'Ma' near Yarcombe in Devon, and Rory is instructed to go in his place. Puzzled by the urgency of the journey, Rory travels the long distance by train, carrying a secret and important letter under a patch on his shirt.

But Mr Cornwallis' 'Ma' is not the kind lady that Rory expects, and he soon finds himself in very different circumstances as a perilous and complex adventure unravels in pursuit of the mysterious 'blue baccy'.

Catherine Cookson has written many popular books for children and adults. She was born in Tyneside, the setting for *Rory's Fortune*, and now lives in Northumberland.

Rory's Fortune was originally published under the title *Blue Baccy*.

Rory's Fortune
by
Catherine Cookson

Futura

Illustrations by Anthony Kerins

A Futura Book

Text copyright © 1972 Catherine Cookson
Illustrations copyright © 1988 Macdonald & Co
(Publishers) Ltd

First published in Great Britain in 1972
under the title *Blue Baccy*,
by Macdonald & Jane's Publishers Ltd

This Futura edition published in 1988 by
Macdonald & Co (Publishers) Ltd
London & Sydney
Reprinted 1988

ISBN 0 7088 4055 8

Reproduced, printed and bound in Great Britain by
Hazell Watson & Viney Limited
Member of BPCC plc
Aylesbury, Bucks, England

Futura Publications
A Division of
Macdonald & Co (Publishers) Ltd
Greater London House
Hampstead Road
London NW1 7QX
A member of Maxwell Pergamon Publishing Corporation plc

CONTENTS

1851

Chapter One

"Now just look at that; did you ever see a finer?" John Cornwallis rubbed his bearded chin, then patted the bark of a yet unstripped oak trunk lying obliquely across the whole length of the yard bordering the wheelwright's shop and house. He patted it as he might do his horse, as if it were a live thing.

Rory McAlister, standing by his master's side, his squarish tousled head held at a jaunty angle, endorsed Mr Cornwallis' words, saying, "No, I never did, Master. What you going to use her for?" He, too, spoke as if the tree were still alive. "Mr Patterson's cart?"

"What!" John Cornwallis turned on the boy. "Patterson's cart! That!" He now thrust his finger towards the oak trunk. "That for a dog cart! No, boy, never! That's going into Farmer Ridley's waggon. 'Twas me father who built the last one and meself who finished my apprenticeship on it. Seven long years I worked afore I was allowed to handle a waggon and then it was Farmer Ridley's. An' that's many a day since. Thirty-three years, lad, Farmer Ridley has been using that waggon. It was made to fit the ruts of the road and it still does. Don't know meself why he wants a new one, but there, who am I to turn down business?" The wheelwright pulled in his lips to suppress a smile, then they both laughed at each other warmly like father and son might have done. Indeed, John Cornwallis looked on the boy almost as a son. His wife too, thought of him almost as her own. If it hadn't been for the lad's devotion to his own family, undoubtedly she would have suggested putting in writing a claim to him. And he himself would have been willing; oh aye, very willing.

"Well now." John Cornwallis jerked his head. "Tomorrow she'll be in the saw pit. I want to get her all done and nicely stacked afore I start me journey. And you go on your journey this day, don't you?"

"Aye, Master," said Rory, "but it won't be as long as yours, me five and your five hundred and more. Eeh!" Rory shook his head. "That's a distance and no mistake, Master, five hundred miles."

"Aye, lad, it's a distance, and no mistake." John Cornwallis turned abruptly away now. The smile had slid from his face and his countenance had taken on the look that was usual to him, a sober look.

From the village of Wind Fell, where John Cornwallis had lived most of his life, to deep into the country of Durham he was known as a sober man, a good man, an upright man, a man who had never been known to do a wrong or underhand thing. Even the parson had spoken of his goodness, and everybody knew that Parson Amery was not for buttering up people. Where, he had said, would you find another man who would travel more than five hundred miles every other year or so to visit his mother who lived far away near a village called Yarcombe in the county of Devon? Where? And no one could answer.

Rory knew exactly where Yarcombe was, although it was too small to be shown on the map. During the four years he had worked for Mr Cornwallis the map had been a source of great interest to Rory. It was on the wall behind the chair and wooden bench on which Mr Cornwallis reckoned up his accounts, and the bench was in the storeroom behind the shop. Rory had wondered why his master did the accounts on the rough old bench, when in the sitting room upstairs there was a beautiful shining desk; then he had discovered that Mr Cornwallis might be master downstairs, but in the house above the shop it was Mrs Cornwallis who ruled. Mrs Cornwallis said the business of the shop must be kept in the shop and when her husband came upstairs, or those with him, there must be no shop talk; upstairs was for eating, and reading, and listening to her playing the harmonium.

Mrs Cornwallis might be a martinet, but she was a kind, motherly martinet. Rory was very fond of her. At times he would feel guilty about his feelings towards both Mr and Mrs Cornwallis because he feared they were ousting his parents from his affections. Although he told himself this could never be possible, he knew that every time he went home on his fortnightly half-day he was always glad to get back to the wheelwright's shop and to them both.

Rory followed his master down the long yard now, past the saw pit, past a stack of elm stocks, and walked round a neat pile of sawn ash felloes which would eventually form part of the rim of a wheel for some waggon, or farm cart, or lady's trap.

Then they entered the wheelwright's shop where Peter Tollett, an old man well into his seventieth year, was lovingly making the hollow belly to a felloe. He was using an adze with the precision of a sculptor, and Rory paused for a minute and looked at him, as he always did, because one day he hoped to be able to make a felloe like Peter, to be able to detect the shakes in the wood, the rind-galls, flaws which you didn't come across until you opened up your tree and discovered them where the bark penetrated deep into the heart of the wood.

Old Peter was finishing this year. Mr Cornwallis was giving him a pension of two shillings a week. It was only one-sixth of his wage but nevertheless it would pay his cottage rent and keep him in bread. That, together with his patch for vegetables, was surely all a man could want?

Rory had wished for a long time now that he were five years older, say twenty, then he might have been able to step into Peter's shoes; but it was nearly sure that Mr Cornwallis would now make Benny Croft full-time and give him Peter's place, although Benny, only half Peter's age, had not his skill

Rory himself had done nearly four years of his apprenticeship and when he entered his fifth year at Christmas he would get two shillings a week. Mr Cornwallis had started him on a wage of sixpence when he first came into the shop; his work then had consisted of chopping the branches of the oaks into cord wood, and the twiggy boughs into small pieces to be sold to the baker for his oven and to a potter in Newcastle for his kiln.

Mr Cornwallis had no need to pay him anything. If apprentices got their bed and board they were lucky. He had always been lucky, at least since he was eleven years old; before that – well, he didn't like to remember what he had done before that, although at nights he had dreams about being a scarecrow again. He could recall scarecrowing from when he was four years old. He did not know at what age he had first started work but he remembered well, when he was seven, his father and mother, young John, Katie and Sarah and himself leaving Hebburn and going to work on a farm; and it had seemed to him that from then on not one of them straightened their backs for years.

It was on the farm that his father had begun to cough and spit blood. The doctor had said to his father that he must have rest and milk and good broth. His father had laughed at the doctor, he had laughed until he had cried. None of them laughed with him but they all cried.

Of his nine brothers and sisters four had died with the cholera a few years back; these were the four that

12

came next to him in age, John, Katie, Sarah and Annie. Now there remained only Bill, who was nine, Sammy seven, Edna five, Mabel three, and the baby, Joseph who was three months old.

For four years now his earnings had been the mainstay of the family. But what was of more value than his wage was the bag of bread and taties Mrs Cornwallis always gave him to take home.

"Upstairs with you," said Mr Cornwallis; "it's your day for home. Have you forgotten?"

Rory grinned as he answered, "No, Master; I couldn't forget that no matter what else I did."

The two men in the shop laughed, and Peter Tollett called after him, "Don't spend all your wage at one go, lad."

Rory did not answer, but went through the back shop and up the narrow stairs to the house above. "Don't spend all your wage at one go." He knew a slight bitterness as he repeated the words to himself. He'd have been glad if his mother could have spared him tuppence, even a penny; he'd had nothing these past two months, and he would like a Sunday coat. By! Aye, he would like a Sunday coat.

"Now, boy, there you are." He was confronted at the kitchen door by Mrs Cornwallis. "Have you washed those hands?" As she picked up one of his hands and looked at the palm he said quickly, "Eeh! I'm sorry, Missis."

"Away, down you go. It should be a habit with you now after all this time. Excited I suppose you are? Well now, hurry yourself." She turned him round and thrust him down the stairs again and he ran out into the yard and to the pump, and there, after filling a pail of water, he washed not only his hands but also his face and neck and the front of his hair, telling himself it would save time after his dinner.

Back upstairs again he looked at Mrs Cornwallis bustling between the trestle table that ran down the

13

centre of the kitchen and the open stove on which a big black pan was boiling, and he said, "I'm spruced, Mrs Cornwallis."

Turning and looking him up and down she said, "Aye, that's better. But as for being spruced, you won't look spruce until you have a new coat and breeches."

Rory dropped his head slightly. It wasn't like Mrs Cornwallis to point out his shabbiness. But then his chin jerked as she ended, "We'll have to see about it, won't we?"

"You mean that, Missis?" His eyes were sparkling.

"I'm not in the habit of saying things I don't mean, you should know that by now. Well, sit up. You're wasting your time; sit up, the longer you stay here the less you'll be able to spend with your family." She now picked up a large soup plate from the table and, going to the pan, she ladled into it stewed mutton and dumplings, and when she placed it before Rory he looked up at her and smiled his thanks.

"Get it down you; it'll stick to your ribs. And the time you're eating I'll go and see what bits and pieces I've got for your mother."

"Oh thanks, Missis." He watched her bustling down the room towards the door that led into the corridor, from which opened the sitting room and the bedrooms and the stairway to the loft. She was small but he thought of her as a cuddly woman, and many was the time during the last year or so that he had felt inclined to hug her by way of thanks for her kindnesses.

He had just finished his meal when she came back into the room and dropped two small sacks on the floor saying, "There now, them's taties." She pointed to one sack. "Enough to fill their bellies for two days, three if they're sparin'. And in there, there's bread, and a dollop of drippin' and a shive of belly pork."

He was on his feet standing near her, his face unsmiling as he looked at her and said, "Ta ... thanks, Mrs Cornwallis. Thanks a lot. Me ma'll be grateful." At odd times, such as now, he addressed her as Mrs Cornwallis; saying her name seemed to express his feelings more fully.

"Well now, on the road with you," she said. "Give your mother my regards. And I hope you find your father better. There, now get yourself away. And put a stout rope sling atween those sacks so they won't scrape your shoulders."

"I will, I will, Missis. Ta, an'thanks. An' bye-bye."

"Bye-bye, lad. And don't be late mind; back here at seven. Don't forget you've got to get up in the morning. Tomorrow will be a long day; Mr Cornwallis wants that oak put in the pit and sliced afore he takes his leave, and that's only three days ahead."

"I know, Missis, an' I won't be late; I'll be up afore me clothes are on, you'll see."

They nodded at each other and smiled, and he went down the stairs, carrying a sack in each hand. But before he made the rope sling for his shoulders, he ran to the storeroom, grabbed up a turnip and dashed out of the back door, which opened on to the common, and ran towards the goat that was tethered to a stake and gasped, "Think I'd forgotten you? Why, you know I wouldn't do that. There, get that into you." He dropped the turnip on the ground, patted the goat, which bleated loudly, then dashed back to the yard.

Five minutes later he left the wheelwright's shop and walked down the main street of the village with the sacks hanging in front of his shoulders. He went past the Grey Hen public house, then, level with Mrs Beeney's house-window-shop, he saw her face and one arm straining round the partition as she tried to place the tray of home-made toffee in front of the window. He paused for a second in his step and looked from the tray to her, then smiled, and her voice came to him, shouting, "Rory! Hold your hand a minute, you Rory!" and he stopped and waited for her coming. When she appeared at the house door she handed him a piece of paper on

15

which lay scranchums from the bottom of a toffee tray, with three whole squares of toffee among them.

"For me? Oh ta, Mrs Beeney."

"Do to chew on your way home, lad."

" Aye, Mrs Beeney. Bye, Mrs Beeney."

"Bye, lad."

She made a lovely taffy, did Mrs Beeney. By! people were kind. But as he turned a bend in the village street he glanced along the road where at the far end stood a blacksmith's shop. Mr Morley Cornwallis wasn't kind. By no! far from it. How on earth he came to be related to his master, he couldn't think. The relationship was a bit stretched, them being only second cousins, and there was no resemblance between them, no more than between chalk and cheese. Mrs Morley Cornwallis, too, was as mean as her husband, and their Bernie took after them both.

As if his thoughts had conjured up Bernie out of thin air, a tall boy came from a passage-way between two houses and stopped for a moment and surveyed him; then grinning at him, he shouted, "Goin' hawkin?"

It was on the tip of Rory's tongue to shout back, "Hawkin'! You watch yourself, else I'll hawk you." But he stopped himself in time. There were two reasons for his restraint: first, the master had warned him against fighting with Bernie; and then there was Lily, Bernie's sister. Lily always got upset when he and Bernie went for each other. He had lost count of the number of fights he'd had with Bernie over the last four years. But lately Mr Cornwallis had said, "You're too big for that now, lad. No more scrapping; you must learn to control your temper and use your head instead of your fists."

It was with this in mind that he now fought his instinct and asked a question as one craftsman might to another. "Plenty in?" he said.

"Plenty in!" Bernie screwed up his face. "What's it to you if we've plenty in or not?"

Count ten, Mr Cornwallis had advised him, then say,

16

God bless us and save us, three times. He counted ten and he had only said God bless us and save us twice, when Bernie shouted, "I asked you what it's got to do with you what we've got in?"

"Nowt. Nowt." Rory was barking back at him now. "I just thought I'd ask, that's all ... That's all."

"Sneaking, more like."

"What need have I to sneak?"

"So's you can go and tell Uncle John what we're doing."

"Aw, don't be so daft, man." Rory glared up at the tall thin figure before him. "He's only to come along the street and look in the forge an' he'll see for himself."

"Then why had you to put your neb in and ask? Playin' the big fellow, eh, bossin' it. Aw, we all know what you're after; sneakin' into Uncle John's good books, toadying to him an' Aunt Rosie. Aw, we all know about you, we do."

"If you don't shut your big mouth there's something more you'll know about me, for I'll ram me fist into it."

"Bernie!"

They both turned and looked towards the opening of the blacksmith's shop and to the leather-aproned man standing there. "Come in here!" Morley Cornwallis jerked his head at his son; then as Rory walked into the road with the intention of crossing to the other side, Morley Cornwallis shouted at him, "That's it, you keep your distance. Trouble-maker you are; there's never a voice raised at this end of the village until you appear on the scene."

Oh, the injustice of it. Rory gritted his teeth. He would have loved to call out, "If ten men in our shop were hammering in felloes they'd still be able to hear you carrying on." Quiet end of the village indeed!

He was on the other side of the road when he passed the blacksmith's open door and he kept his gaze straight ahead while he comforted himself by thinking, jealousy, that's all it is. They were green because Mr Cornwallis had taken him on instead of Bernie. Mr Cornwallis had refused Bernie as an apprentice wheelwright for, as he said, his place was by his father's side, learning his father's trade. But Rory guessed that the real reason why Bernie hadn't been taken on was that Mr Cornwallis didn't like him; and also, his master, being no fool, knew that his half-cousin Morley wanted a sure footing, as it were, in both businesses in the village.

Aw, well – he shrugged the halter rope between the two sacks into a more comfortable position – it was his time off and he wasn't going to worry any more about Morley Cornwallis or Bernie. The sun was shining, there was a high wind blowing, there were four miles of open fell land stretching before him, and he was going home to see his people.

"Rory! Rory!"

He turned and looked at the girl running across a field path that led from the farm, and, smiling, he went to meet her. He rested his sacks on the top of the stone wall that edged the field and watched her skipping over the rough hummocks while she steadied the large can of milk.

She almost fell against the other side of the wall, and after resting for a moment she gasped, "Hello, Rory. You going home?"

"Aye, Lily; it's me time off."

"I thought it was near."

"Aye."

They looked at each other, then nodded; there seemed nothing more to say. But it wasn't often he saw Lily, and he felt he should talk, say something, so he said, "I nearly had a do again with your Bernie."

"Oh no! Rory."

"Aye, well, he gives me the pip. I tried to be civil, I did, Lily, I did. I tried to talk to him, you know? I asked him had he any work in an' you should have heard how he went for me, said I was sneakin'."

Lily made no comment on this but, moving the can on

18

to a flat stone on top of the wall to the side of her, she drew her finger up and down its cool side as she said, "Me ma's takin' me into Shields the morrow; I'm to have a new frock."

"Oh aye! Oh, that's grand."

"I don't want a new frock."

"You don't?" His face was screwed up in surprise. He looked at the top of the dress she was wearing. It was a print, washed colourless with the times it had been in the poss tub. "Why, I would have thought ..."

"Well I don't, I don't! I don't want no new frock."

Her tone caused her face to drop into troubled lines. His eyes widened as he saw her lips tremble. "What is it, Lily? What's up?" he asked quietly.

She was again stroking the side of the can with her finger, and now there was a sound of tears in her voice as she muttered, "Frank Jackson."

"Frank Jackson?" Rory now screwed up his face, trying to associate what Frank Jackson had to do with a new frock and her being near to tears. The only thing he knew about Frank Jackson was that he was a carter and he had lost his wife last year and had three children.

She was looking at him now and her eyes were bright with tears. "He's comin' a courtin'."

"WHAT! ... JACKSON?"

She moved her head once.

"But you can't. He can't; he's old, thirty or more, and he has bairns. Your mother wouldn't –" he paused –"she doesn't want you to, does she?"

She gave him the answer when, with head bent, she repeated, "She's takin' me into Shields to buy me a new frock. Me da gave her the money."

He stared at her, gaped at her. He couldn't believe it. Frank Jackson courting her, Lily. Why, she wasn't sixteen yet, not till next month, she was just his age. He said grimly, "You don't want to, do you?"

She shook her head then wet her finger on the tip of her tongue and traced it round the bottom of the milk

19

can before she said, in a voice scarcely above a whisper, "Ma says I won't have much choice being plain an' that."

"*Plain?*" His voice was deeply indignant. "Your ma said you were plain? She must be up the pole."

She brought her eyes to his; and again they stared at each other before she said, "Ta, Rory. But ... but she's right, I know I am. I'll never be like Betty Howlett or Cissie Macintosh."

"And a good job an' all. Trashy, Betty Howlett is, real trashy. As for Cissie Macintosh, why neither of them can even write their name, you can."

"Aye." She nodded at him, her face pink now with a certain pride and pleasure. "An' I have you to thank for it, Rory. And I've been learnin' me numbers on the quiet. Your da must have been a clever man to have learned you, it's a pity he's sick."

"Aye –" he nodded his head – "it is. But look here. About Frank Jackson. They can't make you, you know that, they can't make you unless you want to. An' he's got three bairns already."

"He's also got three carrier carts, an' he's opening up another line into Newcastle. Six horses and four carts he'll have then, it means a lot to me da."

He leant towards her now, his face almost touching hers as he whispered hoarsely, "But if you stick out, Lily, they can't make you."

"Do you want me to stick out?"

There was a long pause before he said firmly, "Aye. Aye, I do. I don't know how long for, I'll not be out of me time for three years yet, and there's them back home, but ... but I still want you to stick out."

"I'll stick out then, Rory."

He straightened up, reached out and pulled the sacks towards him; then putting the rope halter round his neck he looked at her again as he said, "Well, mind you don't forget what you've just said. Is it a promise?"

"It's a promise, Rory."

They both nodded at each other unsmiling; then he

turned away and walked over the fells.

He felt bigger, tall, not a lad any more. He knew Lily would keep her promise. It might be a stiff fight; it would be, knowing her da.

Another mile on he was climbing a hill, and when he reached the summit there, in the far distance, he could see the masts of the ships on the River Tyne. Away to the far right lay the outskirts of Shields, a great conglomeration of houses. How he wished they could have a house, a decent house, with a wooden floor. Aw, what was the good of wishing that. He hitched the halter farther up on to his shoulders and set off down the hill. By-passing Jarrow, he forked to the left, walking along the banks of a stream; then all of a sudden he was leaving the country and entering the outskirts of Hebburn.

He took a short cut through a labyrinth of small cottages. These were white-washed and bright-looking, they had a prosperous look. The men who lived in them were likely in work in the shipyard at Jarrow, or the pit; anyway, they'd be in work, with a wage coming in regular, as long as they kept their health.

His chin jerked against his thoughts of envy, and he cut sharply across some waste land to where, at the far side in a hollow, stood three cottages as different from those he had passed as could be imagined.

Kelly's Row hadn't been fit for habitation for years but the cottages had never been empty. When one family moved out another was ready to jump in, so quickly it was said that they passed each other in the doorway.

He was about twenty yards from the end cottage when he saw the door pulled violently open and his brother Sammy come dashing out and fly down the road. He paused for a moment before calling, "Sammy! You Sammy!"

Sammy pulled up, looked towards him, and then came tearing over the ground, crying "Rory! Oh our Rory!"

"What is it? What's up? What are you bubbling for?"

Rubbing the tears from the end of his nose with the back of his thumb, the small boy spluttered, "Man ... the man, he's come again; he ... he wants me for a sweep, five pounds he's offerin' now. 'Twas only three day afore yesterday. He keeps on at me ma; he's told her I'll be all right."

Rory didn't listen to any more but started to run towards the house with the boy at his side. "What's me ma up to?" he cried. "Why hasn't she put him out?"

"She's been flat for days, pains in her belly, she's got the runs; she's got to lie down. He ... he grabbed me, Rory. He put the money on the table and he ..."

Rory burst through the door and into the room that was used for all the requirements of living; and on his entry his nose didn't wrinkle, as it usually did from the smell, the smell of sickness and the water from the middens that continuously seeped under the stone floor and came up through the cracks, the smell of clothes never really washed and never really dried, the overall smell of dire poverty; and he glared at the man.

His entrance had caused a sudden silence in the hubbub. His da was leaning on his elbow, his breath coming in tight, painful gasps as he tried to speak; his mother was sitting at the foot of the pallet bed, her arms around her stomach; his five-year-old sister Edna, and Mabel, who was three, were crouched one on each side of her, and the baby, Joseph, who was but three months old, lay almost inert in the basket to the side of the dying fire.

"What you after?" Rory let the sacks slip slowly from his shoulders down to the floor, but he held on to the halter as if he would swing them upwards again to the man's head.

The man, a stocky, stunted individual with an unusually long face and high forehead, which part of him did not seem to match his body, now asked with a sneer, "Who you when you're out, youngster?"

22

"Never mind who I am, get yourself out of here, an' quick, else I'll kick you out!"

"Kick me out, huh! Now look you here; I've come to do this family a good turn. Just look at them. If ever I saw anybody in need of a shillin' or two it's them. An' I'm tellin' you, he'd go to a good man; I know him as if he was me brother. Doesn't go in for factory flues nor the big mansions where the lads get stuck in the crannies, he's thoughtful he is; small flues, that's his business, small flues. An' the young 'uns take pride in doin' a good job. Why, he even carries them from one chimney to another so's they make no dirt in the house, an' the housewife always appreciates this, with special tit-bits for the lads. I'm tellin' you, he'll go a lot farther and fare worse, an' he'll not get another offer like this again."

"And I'm tellin' you –" Rory moved towards him now, his body bent, his head thrust out – "I'm tellin' you to get out of here afore I kick you out and then call the constable. You know as well as I do it's against the law to take any lad under ten, unless he's willing." So ferocious was his manner that the man backed towards the door. Nevertheless, he still looked as if he were going to continue the argument, until Rory said, "I'll give you two ticks to get into the street!"

"You, you young snipe, talkin' of constables. I'll have you up afore the Justices for threatenin'."

"You do that, you do that, and then you can explain how you're goin' round buyin' lads, and it against the law, you do that, mister, you do; go on!" He drew his arm backwards, his fist doubled, and the man went out, but not without having the last word. "I'll see me day with you," he growled at him through his teeth. "Trying to play the big fellow you are, an' your folks stinkin' and starvin'."

Rory now gripped the door and banged it in the man's face and had the satisfaction of hearing him yell; then he turned and looked at his family, and they at him.

24

Peter McAlister was thirty-eight years old but he looked sixty. His thick mop of dark hair accentuated the bony pallor of his face, his hand, where it gripped the side of the flock mattress, was like a claw, and his body was so emaciated that it gave no evidence of itself under his rough nightshirt.

Jane McAlister was thirty-four. She had borne ten children. Bill, who was nine, came next to Rory, and was the only other member of the family who was working. His wage was more than Rory's, being one and nine a week, and at times going up to as much as two and threepence, but then he had to be kept out of it, and it was the keeping that was the main thing; keeping Edna and Mabel and the bairn fed – her man didn't eat much, not of the food she could give him anyway.

She bowed her head now against Rory's stare, for his eyes seemed to be probing deep into hers and seeing there how nearly she had succumbed to the temptation of taking the five pounds that the man had offered for Sammy. She had refused it four times within the last week, but she knew she couldn't go on refusing it; and the man had known that too.

Her weary gaze dropped towards the two sacks lying on the floor, and she noticed immediately that they were fuller than usual and she thanked God. She looked up at her eldest son, and then said, "Hello, lad."

"Hello, Ma."

Rory now walked slowly to the bed and looked at his father who had lain back. "Hello, Da, how you keepin'?" he asked.

"Oh, much the same, lad, much the same."

The two children scrambled off the bed and gripped his hands and he looked from one to the other and smiled and said, "Hello Mabel. Hello Edna," and they answered, "What you brought us, Rory?"

He turned swiftly away from them and, lifting the sacks from the floor, emptied the bread and belly pork on to the table. The sight of it brought Jane McAlister to her feet, and when she reached the table she stared down at the good food as if looking upon gold dust.

'Them's taties –'' Rory pointed to the other sack – ''enough to last you a week if you go steady with them. An' I'll bring the same along next week.''

''You're gettin' a holiday every week?'' His mother was looking at him; and looking straight back into her eyes he lied and said, ''Aye, aye; every week.'' His mind was working rapidly. When he got back he'd go to his master and put it to him. He'd ask him if he could split his half-day so that he could visit home once a week; and then he'd put it to the mistress, in a nice way of course, that he'd do owt she wanted after half-past seven at night, such as scrubbin' down the stairs or possing the master's rough cords and the heavy bedding. Oh, there were a dozen and one jobs he could do extra in payment for a couple of sacks every week. And his mind racing on told him there was another thing he must do; but that would keep until just before he was leaving, so that there'd be less argument.

''Get some water, Edna,'' he said, ''and then put the tatie pot on the fire.'' Turning to his mother and pointing to the belly pork, he added, ''Will I boil this or fry it, Ma?''

''Oh, fry it, lad; it'll be quicker. But I can do it.''

''No, you go and sit yourself down, I'll see to it . . .''

Half-an-hour later, with the exception of Peter, they were all sitting round the table, not gobbling the food as one would have expected, but eating slowly, savouring every mouthful, glancing every now and then at each other and smiling. Even Peter, from the bed, was smiling. His eating was even slower than that of the rest and punctuated by coughing, but he was smiling. At one point he said, ''You're not havin' any, lad?''

''No, Da; I had me nuff afore I came away, I'm choked up.''

''That's good then, that's good.'' Peter nodded towards Rory; then asked, ''You're still liking it there?''

26

It was odd, Rory thought, that his father should ask this question almost every time they met, but he answered in the same vein, "Oh aye, Da; it's the best place on earth." And, as always, he added, "There's no master like Mr Cornwallis, he's a good man."

"Yes, he's a good man."

They nodded at each other.

When the meal was over and the table cleared, Rory sat by his father's side, and still keeping to the pattern, told him the doings in the wheelwright's shop, while the children knelt on the clippie mat at his feet and his mother lay down once more on the pallet bed.

After a while Rory got up and went to the door and looked into the sky to see where the sun was. When he came back into the room he said, "Well, it's me for the road, Da." Then he paused and, going close to the bed, looked at his father; and again he said, "Da," and Peter, looking up at him, asked, "Aye, lad, what is it?"

"I'm ... I'm goin' to take Sammy back with me, 'cos I don't trust that bloke." He couldn't say that he couldn't trust his mother's strength to hold out against five golden sovereigns. He watched his father and mother exchange glances, then his father was looking at him again, saying to him, "You do that, lad, But what will you do with him? He's too young to be apprenticed."

"The master'll find something for him, I'm sure of that. If not, there's always a bit of field work. An' he can sleep along of me. I'll arrange it with the mistress about his feed." He spoke with more confidence than he was feeling at the moment, for he knew that although his mistress was kind, there was such a thing as taking advantage of a good nature.

Sammy, who had been sitting on the floor, was now on his feet. "Me goin' along of you, Rory, to the shop?"

"Aye, to the shop."

"An' I can stay there?"

His voice had ended on a high note, almost a squeak, and Rory said, "Aye, you can stay there, providing you don't turn lazy." He cuffed his brother's ear, and Sammy giggled and began to laugh almost hysterically as he danced about the room, pushing first at Edna and then at Mabel, crying, "I'm goin' with our Rory! I'm goin' to the shop I am! I am!"

"Can I come an' all, Rory?" Edna was standing looking up at him with her great brown eyes, and he touched her cheek gently as he said, "No, you stay and look after our ma and da. And I tell you what, I'll bring you some flowers . . . heather next time."

Edna nodded, swallowed deeply, then turned away; and Rory said, "Now, come on young 'un." Then more quietly, as he looked at his father, he murmured, "Good-bye, Da. I hope you'll get on better this week."

"Good-bye, lad; I'm doing fine." They nodded at each other. Then Rory stood looking at his mother. Somehow the sight of her made him want to cry. She had once been bonny; when he was very young he had known she had been bonny, but now she looked old, and unwashed, and she smelt of sick. "Bye-bye, Ma." He put out his hand, and she took it and gripped it tightly as she said; "Bye-bye, lad. And thanks, thanks, for, for your pay an' everything."

He moved swiftly to the door with Sammy at his heels; but stopped before he reached it and he turned on his younger brother and cried, "Say bye-bye then."

"Oh aye." Sammy swung round now and ran to the bed and said, "Bye, Da."

"Bye, me bairn," said Peter thickly, tousling his son's hair.

"Bye, Ma."

"Bye, son." His mother put her fingers under his chin and lifted his face up to hers and looked down into it for a long moment before saying, "Be a good lad, now."

"Aye, Ma, I will." He now, in his mercurial way, turned to Edna, who was as tall as him although two years younger. "Ta-rah, our Edna."

"Ta-rah, Sammy." Edna again swallowed.

28

"Ta-rah, our Mabel." Sammy could bend to Mabel, and Mabel grinned up at him and said, "Ta-rah, our Sammy."

The farewells over, he dashed up to where Rory was standing in the doorway and grabbed at the bottom of his coat, and Rory gave one last look back into the kitchen, then walked away.

Rory kept up a good pace until he was clear of the streets and in the open country again, and not until he became aware of Sammy's gasping breath did he slacken his speed. He had not spoken to the boy since they had left the house but now, looking down at him, he said roughly, "Mind you, you'll have to pull your weight. Do you hear?"

"Aye, Rory."

"And do what you're told, an' no sleepin' in the mornin'. You're a thick head, you know, and like your bed too much."

"Aye, Rory; but I'll get up, first call I'll get up."

"You'd better, you'd better."

The worry in his mind caused his pace to quicken again. Perhaps he had bitten off more than he could chew. Big head, he chastised himself; that's what he was, nowt but a big head, always rushing into things. Two things he had rushed into today; making Lily promise to stick out and wait for him, and now bringing their Sammy to the shop without a by your leave, or if I may? or, is it all right with you? Eeh! he was in for something when he got back, he knew that. He started on Sammy again. "And don't you think you'll get any pay, 'cos you won't, not for years an' years. Lucky if you get your keep an' a bed. And when you do start your apprenticeship, that's if you do, it'll be seven years. You know that? Seven years."

Sammy gazed up at Rory. His face solemn, his eyes wide, he nodded, for he hadn't the breath now to say, "Aye, Rory," his short legs were tired, he was all out of puff.

"And you'll have to keep your eyes and ears open an' learn about wood. In a wheelwright's shop you have to learn about wood. Wood has got ways with it, like women. That's what Mr Cornwallis says. You can get ash that's like a steel hawser and ash that's as boast inside as a big-mouthed galoot. An' you find the same in beech. Aye, and in oak an' all. An' there's somethin' else I'll tell you. If you ever see oaks growing in a valley, well, you leave 'em there. Do you hear? Leave 'em there."

Now Sammy drew in a deep breath and on a gasp said, "Aye, Rory, aye, I'll leave 'em there."

"You do."

What was he on about, talkin' about wood to a bairn? What would the bairn know about wood for years ahead? He was only just coming by the knowledge himself. He was all wound up; that was why he was acting as he was. And he had run the bairn off his legs. Suddenly he stopped and looked down at Sammy and asked quietly, "You tired?"

Sammy blinked up at him, then said, "No, Rory. No, I'm not tired."

The look on Sammy's face belied his words, and Rory was about to say, "Don't be frightened, nothing will happen to you, you'll be all right," but not being sure of this he remained silent and walked on, but much slower now.

If anybody was frightened at this minute he told himself, he knew who it was. Crickey Moses! he was the one for pushing his luck, wasn't he?

Half-an-hour later he approached the end of the village street and he knew something odd was afoot. There was a stir about the place, never evident at this time of day. A number of men were standing outside the Grey Hen; one was Farmer Armstrong, and another, old Doctor Bennett's driver.

The men stopped their conversation and looked at him as he passed them; but they didn't speak to him, and he blinked in slight embarrassment and hurried on.

30

Mrs Beeney was outside her shop talking to Miss Tyler, who made dresses and things. They, too, looked at him, but didn't speak. He wondered for a moment if it was because he had Sammy hanging on to him.

When he entered the wheelwright's yard there was the doctor's gig standing in the middle of it, and there was also Morley Cornwallis talking in his loud blustering voice to Peter Tollett and Benny Croft. He had his hand raised, wagging it as if he were threatening them, at least admonishing them, and they were staring back at him both grim-faced.

Morley turned and, catching sight of Rory, called, "So you're back, are you, you're back?"

"Aye, I'm back, and afore me time."

"Cheek! Give me your cheek, would you? Get going! By! if I had . . ."

"Morley!" It was Mrs Cornwallis calling from the doorway. Her face looked grim, but white, very white, and her voice was low as she said, "I'll thank you to keep your voice down, Morley. And if there's orders to give I'm capable of giving them; until John's on his feet again."

"Now! Rosie, Rosie." Morley was moving towards her. "I was only saying . . ."

"I know what you were saying, Morley. But you heard what I said. When I need you I'll send for you."

"You're insulting me, Rosie."

"Not my intention, Morley, to insult you. All I'm asking is for you to go now and leave us in peace. Come in, boy, come in." She put out her hand and hastily drew Rory with Sammy attached to him into the back shop. Then closing the door she looked from him to Sammy and asked, "Who is this?"

"Me brother, Mrs Cornwallis."

"What's he doing here?"

"Well, it's like this. But Ma'am, afore I tell you will you tell us what's happened to the master?"

Mrs Cornwallis lifted the corner of her apron and

31

wiped her hands on it before she said. "He's had an accident. It happened in the saw pit. He wouldn't wait, he just wouldn't wait; he wanted to get it all sliced and stacked. It's always the way afore a journey, always the way." She now brought her apron up to her face and wiped the sweat from her brow. "It's his back," she said. "The doctor's with him now; we'll know shortly, we'll know shortly."

"Oh! Missis." Rory was finding it difficult to speak. "I'm sorry. If I had been here perhaps I could have . . ."

"You could have done nothing, boy. As I said, when Mr Cornwallis has a journey in front of him he's always agitated, always, always." She now began a movement with her hands as if washing them; then looking down at Sammy, who was staring wide-eyed at her, she said, "Now tell me now, what is he doing here?"

Standing meekly before her, Rory told Mrs Cornwallis why he had brought his brother, ending, "I'll do anything, Missis, anything; take all the rough I will. An' he can work, he can an' all; he's small, but he's quick to learn." He stopped for a moment before saying, his voice very quiet, "I couldn't bear to know him bein' pushed up the chimneys. Awful that is. They choke to death. There was a lad burned, burned alive 'cos they couldn't get at him . . ."

Mrs Cornwallis was wagging her hand at him, her head was bent and her eyes tightly closed as she said, "Enough! boy. Enough. Well, we'll have to sort this out after. In the meantime he can have his bed and board and make himself useful. But it's not for me to say yes or no, it'll be the master's decision. You understand that?"

"Yes, Missis. Aw yes, Missis. But he'll be helpful; I can . . ."

"Enough. Enough, I said boy. I must go up again." She went towards the stairs at the far end of the room; then pausing and looking over her shoulder, she said, "Take him to the pump before you put him into bed."

"Yes, Missis." Rory now hustled Sammy outside and

to the pump, and there he whispered hoarsely, "Strip off."

"What! all me clothes?"

"Well, keep your trousers on but off with the others. An' I'll wash your shirt, it'll be dry by mornin'. Put your head down and don't yell when the water hits you."

Sammy didn't yell when the spate of cold water hit the back of his neck but he nearly fainted through shock and weariness.

Ten minutes later, his body pink from the rubbing with a coarse sacking towel but still shivering, he followed Rory through the back room and up the stairs. When they reached the living room Mrs Cornwallis was standing near the table, the corner of her apron once again in her hand. She turned her gaze from the door at the far end of the room and looking at Sammy, she said, "That's better." Then nodding at Rory, she added, "Cut him a chunk of bread and a dollop of pease-pudding –" she jerked her head now towards a side table on which were laid out the eatables that would be served for supper – "then off to bed with him. But you, I . . . I want you down here."

"Yes, Missis." Rory cut a slice of bread from a new loaf and put a tablespoonful of pease-pudding on it, and all the while Mrs Cornwallis stood by the table looking towards the far door. Yet nothing seemed to escape her, for without turning her head she said, "You needn't be stingy, give him another dollop. An' you can cut him a slice of brawn."

"Yes, Missis; thanks, Missis."

When Sammy was only halfway through his meal the far door opened and the doctor, coming into the room, closed it after him. He glanced at the two boys, then said to Mrs Cornwallis, "Come downstairs a minute, will you?" and on this he marched out of the room. Mrs Cornwallis followed him.

They had no sooner gone than Sammy, putting the knife and spoon down on to the plate, looked up at Rory and said, "I can't eat no more, Rory."

"You can't eat that, that good food?"

"It's made me full up."

"Give it here." Rory picked up the plate quickly and finished off the food before saying, "The missis would be vexed to see good food left on the plate. You'll have to learn to eat everything she puts afore you. But there —" he looked down at the weary face and added gently, "Likely you will; it's all strange. Come on." He held out his hand and led Sammy out into the passage and pushed him up the steep ladder into the loft, and there, having tucked him up in the pallet bed on the floor, he knelt for a moment beside him and whispered, "All right?"

"Aye, Rory. Do ... do you think she'll let me stay?"

"I hope so, but as she says, it'll rest with the master. I've got to go now, so go to sleep."

"Aye, Rory ... Rory?"

"Yes, what is it?"

Sammy moved his head on the pillow and his eyelids blinked and the muscles of his face jerked as if he had the tick before he said, "Ta for bringin' me."

"Aw you!" Rory pushed gently at the top of his brother's head, then got up swiftly and left the attic.

When he entered the living room he saw that the bedroom door was partly open and he heard Mr Cornwallis's voice saying, "Give over, woman, give over, I've got to think," then Mrs Cornwallis's voice answering, "And I've got to think an' all; I've got to think for you. You're in a bad way, you know that. Oh! that this should happen. Are you in pain?"

"No, no, I'm not in pain. I wish I was; I wish I could feel my back, but I can feel nothing; once I can feel I'll know there's hope for me. But that's not worrying me at the moment."

Now Mrs Cornwallis's voice said slowly and emphatically, "If you can't go, you can't go."

"Woman, if I can't go then *somebody's* got to go."

34

Rory found himself staring towards the door. He knew he shouldn't be listening but there was a desperate urgency in his master's tone that kept his ears stretched. Then his mistress said two words. She said them with such force, such bitterness that he was startled.

The words were "*blue baccy.*"

Then she repeated them. "*blue baccy!*" she said again, and it was as if she were swearing, cursing.

The master was speaking quietly now, saying, "Somebody's got to go, woman."

"You could send a letter." The mistress's voice had a pleading note in it.

"Not to her I couldn't. Anyway, a letter wouldn't be able to carry it back, would it?"

"She would understand this once."

"No, no; not Ma."

The master was talking about his mother. It was his mother he travelled to the other side of the country to see. He was a dutiful son; the men at the shop, everyone in the village knew he was a dutiful son, but his mother mustn't be a very nice woman if she wouldn't take any notice of a letter and understand he had hurt his back and couldn't come.

His master's voice was very low now and he could only catch a few words here and there, such as, "No, no. God sakes! woman, I couldn't trust Morley." Then his mistress's voice talking rapidly and ending, "You may have to." Then the master again, "Never! Nor one of his house. I . . . I've got to think."

The conversation became muttered and too low for Rory to follow, and as the thought came to him that the missis would be very vexed if she found him, with his lugs cocked as it were, he was about to turn away when there she was standing in the open doorway looking at him. He felt the colour flushing up over his body and right up to his head as if he had been caught doing something really bad.

"I've . . . I've put him to bed, Missis. I've . . . I've just come down to see what you want doin'."

Rose Cornwallis looked at him as she walked down the length of the room and to the table and she continued to stare at him without speaking while the colour deepened in his face and he stammered, "Is ... is the master bad, real bad, Missis?"

Mrs Cornwallis now closed her eyes for a moment and made a small motion with her hand. It was as if she had been dozing and had just come awake, and she said quite quietly, and gently, "Yes, boy, he's bad, very bad."

"Can I do anything, Missis?"

"Yes, boy, yes, yes, I think you can. But first of all, get yourself some food. Then get off to bed."

"Yes, Missis; yes, I'll do that. But ... but if you want me to stay up, sit with the master I will, I'm not tired, not a bit."

"Thanks, boy, I may take you at your word. But do as I bid you now; if I need you I'll call."

"Aye, Missis. I'll be waiting."

Again she said, "Thanks, boy," and they stared at each other for a moment before he turned away and went downstairs.

Chapter Two

Rory was woken from a deep sleep and a wonderful dream, in which he had been loading the furniture from the stinking cottage in Hebburn onto a handcart; and although it was only a small handcart he had laid his parents' pallet bed on it, his father still lying there. He had packed the children round the edges, even Bill, who, under ordinary circumstances, would surely have been in the blacking factory while it was daylight; but there he was perched on the tail end of the handcart. They were going to a new home, and the new home had wooden floors.

"Aye? Yes? Oh! Oh! Missis. Do ... do you want me?" he stammered, blinking and peering up through the candlelight at Mrs Cornwallis, and she whispered, "Yes, boy. But come quietly; don't disturb the youngster."

"Is the master worse?"

"No worse, no better, boy. There now, come along. It doesn't matter about your coat, I'll give you a blanket to put round you." In the living room she stopped and, putting her hand on his shoulder, said, "Your master is not asleep, but he wants to talk to you, and very serious talk. Listen carefully, boy, and you won't lose by it, you understand? He has a great opinion of you, boy, a warm

37

liking." The words brought a swelling into his throat; but it was a comfortable swelling, not the choking kind.

"Come now." She led the way into the bedroom, and Rory followed her slowly to the big four-poster bed in which the master was lying.

When the door closed behind her John Cornwallis made a small movement with his hand and he said, "Turn the chair, boy, so that you're looking at me squarely."

Rory did as he was bid; then he became embarrassed, for the master didn't speak but just lay staring at him.

He had come to the stage when he didn't know where to put his hands and was about to place them in between his knees, as he often did when lost for words, when his master said something that made him forget everything else. "You'll remember this night for as long as you live, boy," he said. "When you're an old man you'll look back on it and you'll say to your children, it started then, that night sitting by me master's bedside."

Rory blinked rapidly. He could say nothing. He had no idea what the master was on about.

"Do you like me, boy?"

"Aw aye, Master. Yes, very much I like you." He could say this without hesitation.

"Would you do me a service if you could?"

"Yes, Master. I think you know that, 'cos I owe you a great deal. If there's any way I can pay you back I will, an' like a shot."

"There's a way you can pay me back, boy; oh, yes, there's a way you can pay me back." The master's eyes were closed now and his head was moving slowly. When he opened his eyes again there was a look of deep pain in them, and he said, "There's no real black in this world and there's no real white. I'm not referring to the colour of a man's skin, boy, but to a man's character. Remember that, remember those words. No soul is really black, and no soul is really white."

"Aye, Master." It was on the point of Rory's tongue to

say, "I think your soul's white, Master." But then you didn't say things like that, you only thought them.

"You know I was to make a journey the day after the morrow, don't you?"

"Aye, Master."

"Where was I going?"

"Where was you going?" Rory jerked his chin sideways, then said, "Where you always go, Master, when you make a long journey, down to the West Country, right across the land to the West Country to visit your mother."

"Aye, right across the land to the West Country to visit my mother ... But I can't go, can I?"

Rory said nothing to this.

"So I'm going to send you in my stead."

"Me, Master?"

"You, Rory."

"Right across the country?"

"Right across the country."

Rory made to get up from his chair. He half raised himself by gripping the arms, then sat down again; and now he did put his joined hands between his knees and rocked his body backwards and forwards two or three times before he said, "You want me to take a message to your mother?"

"... Yes, Rory."

After staring at the master for a moment Rory glanced towards the lamp on the table to the left of him, then he looked down at his hands. Why couldn't the master send the message by letter? It could get there as quick as him, quicker maybe.

"Boy, give me your hand."

Rory pulled his hands from between his knees and extended one towards his master and felt the hard fingers wind round his and grip them. Presently, while they both gazed at each other, John Cornwallis said, in a voice that was not without a tremor, "Boy, I don't know how long I've got to live. If what has happened to my

back is what I think has happened, I could lie here for ten years, or just ten days. But however long I've got of life I'm entrusting it to you this night. From now on you'll hold my life in your hands. Do you understand me?"

No, Rory did not understand him. "You talk, Master," he said, "as if you were in trouble, real trouble."

"You've said the right words, boy. I am in trouble, real trouble."

Rory's face puckered. 'You hold my life in your hands,' the master had said, yet of one thing he was certain, whatever trouble the master was in it wasn't of his own making. But he was speaking again. "Tomorrow early you'll go into Newcastle and you'll buy yourself a good suit of clothes, boy, and an overcoat and stout boots and stockings. Now listen carefully. I'll tell it to you slowly what you have to do, but I'll also write it down on paper so you can't go wrong."

The master now lay silent for some minutes and the only sound in the room was the gasping of his breath; then slowly he said, "You'll take the train from Newcastle to York . . ."

"The train, Master! Go in one of them?"

"Listen, boy." The master's words came slower still. "Before we see each other again you may have travelled by stranger ways than in a railway carriage."

"Aye, Master." Rory swallowed deeply.

"You will go by York to London. Now everything will be straightforward from here to London. It is from there that the journey may be difficult. It is three years since I went that way, and then it was all stops and starts and changes. However, you will finally get by train to Axminster, an' from there you'll take a slow coach to your destination . . ."

"To your mother's house, Master?" Rory's voice was eager, but as he watched his master lift his hand and cover his eyes he shook his head at himself — he should keep his mouth shut and listen and not interrupt his master.

The master now went on: "The house is called 'St Helier's House' and the name of my ... the lady is Ma ... Miss ... Mrs Bluett."

Mrs Bluett! Rory's lips formed the name but he didn't speak it aloud. The master's mother; she'd surely be called Cornwallis, not Bluett. But then, she could have married again. Aye, that was it.

The master had now taken his hand from his eyes and was looking at him and the look disturbed him. He felt forced to enquire, "Are you in pain, Master?"

"No, boy, not as you know pain." His hand came out again, and once more Rory's was gripped between the work-worn bony fingers.

"Can I trust you, boy?"

"With me life, Master. I've said it."

"Aye, an' I know it. I trust you, boy, as I would me own flesh and blood. It may come as news to you, boy, but I look upon you as my flesh and blood, an' if it wasn't that you already have a mother and father, and your loyalty is to them, the missis and I would have long since taken you completely into our home."

Rory's head moved slightly from side to side. He could find no words with which to express his feelings. Then Mr Cornwallis spoke again.

"If you had one wish in the whole world, what would it be, boy? Tell me truthfully at this moment."

Rory's head stopped moving. He stared back into the grey face on the pillow and he had no hesitation in voicing his wish. "A home for me people, Master, that's me one and only wish, a real home with wooden floors and away from the muck of the town; they need fresh air."

Mr Cornwallis looked at him for a long while; then he said, "When you come back, boy, your wish will be granted. Whether I am alive or dead, I'll see it is granted."

"Oh, Master!" It was Rory's hand that went out now and diffidently touched his master's arm, and Mr

Cornwallis patted it for a moment, then cut off Rory's stammering thanks by saying in a low voice, "There are lots of things I could explain to you but they would only befuzzle your brain – and you'll have enough to puzzle you on the journey, for it will all be strange to you. But listen now, and listen carefully. If anyone should enquire of you where you are bound for, you're visitin' your grannie ... your grandmother ..."

"Me grandmother?" Rory coughed, then moved his head down, and Mr Cornwallis repeated, "Your grandmother, boy. That is the tale you will tell until you reach Axminster. Should you be asked from there on what you are about, just say you're on your way to St Helier's House, and nobody will trouble you further. Once there say what you know, I've had an accident, and I'm in me bed unable to move me limbs. From then on say nothing. Keep your mouth shut except when you've got to open it for politeness or eating. You get my meaning?"

Rory nodded slowly.

"You may have to stay put for a while, say a couple of days; then you'll be given a package, perhaps two, to bring back ... Now ... *Now, this is the important part of your journey, boy, for whatever happens, whatever happens, nobody must know what you're carrying until you're in this room again, you understand?*"

"Aye, Master." He could say "Aye, Master," but he didn't understand the half of it, no not half of it; fact was, none of it.

John Cornwallis now said, "I understand you've brought your wee brother back with you to save him from the chimneys; it was a thoughtful deed, an' you can rest your mind on it. At seven he's of an age to make himself useful; there'll be work found for him, never fear."

"Thank you, Master."

"Go now, boy, for it'll soon be light. Wash yourself well, an' eat well, an' –" he paused – "bring your shirt

43

down to the missis; she'll want to put a patch or two on it."

"Me ... me shirt, Master? But ... but it's the one the missis made for me; it's good an' ..."

"The safest place to carry a letter is under a patch, boy; an' that goes for money too an' all."

"... Oh! Oh, aye, Master. Aye, you're right."

"I'll see you afore you go, boy."

"Yes, Master." Rory rose from his chair and walked backwards down the side of the bed, then he turned and went hastily from the room.

Mrs Cornwallis was standing in the kitchen as if she had never moved since the moment he had left her, and when Rory came to her side she said softly, "Well, boy?"

"I'm to go on a journey for the master, Missis."

"Yes, boy." She nodded her head three times before adding, "And you won't lose by it, ever. Bring me your shirt down now."

"Yes, Missis."

As he turned towards the door her voice stopped him. "The master's a good man," she said.

He stared at her, his mouth slightly agape, before he confirmed her words, saying, "Yes, Missis, I know he's a good man."

. . .

The dawn was fast breaking, the light was seeping through the attic window, and Rory was ready to go.

Sammy stood beside him. His face white, his brown eyes looking like those of a startled seal, he gazed up at Rory and asked, "But will the goat not butt me?"

"No, I've told you, she's tame. But for goodness sake remember to see that she's well tied up; keep your eye on the ground stake, she's not called Scapegoat for nothing. You just call Scape! Scape! and she'll come to you."

"And she won't butt?"

44

"No, she won't butt; it's a nanny not a billy. She's as gentle as a kid. Only once she's off the tether she'll be away over the fells an' somebody'll have to go right to the Inn at Gateshead, and the master'll get mad; she always makes her way back to the inn, 'cos she remembers the beer she used to get. So you remember. An' besides that, remember all I've told you an' be a good lad an' do everything the missis says."

"Aye, Rory. Will you be long gone?"

"Aw," Rory's tone was casual-sounding, indicating more confidence than he felt, "Might be a week."

The thought of being away a week suddenly reminded him that Lily wouldn't know where he'd gone. Bending down to Sammy now, he said hastily. "There's a lass at the end of the village, the blacksmith's daughter, if you see her on the quiet, just say to her, Rory said he'll only be gone a few days, might be a week. Will you do that?"

"Aye, Rory. Is she a big lass?"

"About the size of me. Her hair is staight and black an' tied back in a bun, an' they call her Lily. You'll know her."

"Aye, Rory."

"And remember an' all that if I'm not back come Saturday the missis'll put you on the carrier cart with some taties an' things, and tell them at home I won't be long. Now you've got all that?"

Sammy nodded, and Rory put his hand on his brother's head and said, "That's a good lad." Following which, they stared at each other until Rory said abruptly, "Well, come on then."

He went down the ladder first, then put up his hand to guide the short legs reaching for the rungs. When they entered the kitchen Mrs Cornwallis, pointing to the table, said to Sammy, "Sit up and get your bite, boy, afore you start your work. Have you said good-bye to your brother?"

"Yes, Ma'am ... Missis."

"That's a good boy ... Come along, Rory."

45

With a backwards glance towards the face turned towards him, Rory followed Mrs Cornwallis down the stairs and out into the yard, and there, looking at him, she said, "You should get the first carrier cart from the crossroads and you'll be in Newcastle in under the hour." She smiled faintly. "It's a good job you're not starting out the morrow, St Crispin's Day, else you'd wear your shoes out."

"Aye, Missis."

The smile went from her face. "Now, boy, don't forget all you've been told. Don't let the shirt off your back; besides the letter, I've sewn four half-sovereigns into the patches under the oxters. Should you be waylaid, an' I wouldn't put it past the folk who travel on trains, you'll not be destitute; you'll have enough to get you there, and once there they'll see to you coming back. But let's pray to God that nothing such will befall you. God speed, boy. You know what to do . . . And boy . . ."

"Yes, Missis?"

"Always remember what I've said afore, the master is a good man."

To Rory's astonishment his mistress bent swiftly forward and placed her lips on the side of his cheeks before turning and hurrying, almost at a run, back into the wheelwright's shop.

And so he started on his journey not thinking of what lay before him, but only that the missis had kissed him, and had emphasized once again that the master was a good man – well, he had always known that, hadn't he?

Chapter Three

H is buttocks were sore. He felt that his bones were sticking through his skin, in fact his whole body was aching; as he put it to himself, he wouldn't have felt any worse if he had been laced to a cart wheel. He never wanted to ride in a train again as long as he lived. He felt he had been riding in trains for weeks or months, not just for two days. How many trains had he been in? Four, five; he had lost count, and he had long since given up reckoning the number of stations.

The first part of the journey, to York, he had found exciting, but then he had only been sitting on the wooden seat for a matter of a few hours or so and he had been wedged between a plump man and an equally plump woman, and they had cushioned the jogging for him.

But at York, Rory had lost his two companions, and with them, the warmth of their bodies. In spite of his new suit and thick melton cloth overcoat he had shivered for the remainder of the journey to London, for although the compartment was packed, his close travelling companions were two thin ladies, one of whom complained about three unruly children present and certainly didn't whisper when, addressing herself to no one in particular, she said that children should not be allowed to travel second class but should be made to go third; sixteen shillings and eightpence she had paid to suffer this.

Mr Cornwallis had written down the address of a hostelry in London, where he was to stay the night; the place was close to the station. But when, stiff with cold and weary, he emerged from the station, the sight that confronted him made him forget his discomfort. He had never seen so many people together or so much traffic in all his life ... and at night time! There were horse-drawn trams, and cabs of all shapes and sizes; the whole scene was utterly bewildering.

The hostelry, a very ordinary one, appeared grand to Rory, though the meal he was served was, he knew, not a patch on what Mrs Cornwallis would have cooked. But he was too tired and weary to mind much. After eating he went straight to his room, in which was a wash-hand-stand with a basin and a ewer on it, and the water in the ewer had the chill off it. It was all very grand, he thought.

He went to bed in his shirt, as he always did, but with one difference, he kept it buttoned right up to the neck and went to sleep with his arms folded across his chest ...

He had thought the journey from York very harassing, but before he had been a few hours on the road to the West Country he was looking back with nostalgia on his first introduction to the railway.

At times he had a corner seat, when he could look out at the countryside, which here was different altogether from what it had been on the other side of London. And then those people who did speak to him were hardly understandable, like foreigners, and he, he realized, must appear the same to them. Unlike the kind man who had asked him to repeat slowly what he had said, most of them smiled or guffawed when he opened his mouth, and always asked what part of the world he was from. He had become peeved and for most of the long tedious journey kept his mouth shut.

Now he understood there were only ten more miles to go. For two days Rory hadn't done a hand's turn of work, just sat and sat, yet now he was more tired than he used to be when he did twelve hours in the blacking factory and had to walk the four miles home afterwards.

"Where be you for, boy?"

"What?"

"I said where be you for? Not deaf are you?"

"No, no, I'm not deaf." Where be you for? He was in a world of foreigners. Aw! he saw now what the man was getting at. "I'm for the Axminster station."

"Oh aye. But where be you for after that?"

"I'm going to see me ... me grandmother."

"Your grandmother? And where be she?"

"Wha ... Oh ... er ... well, it's a place atween the station and a village called Yarcombe I'm told."

"You're told? Don't you know? never been afore?"

"No."

"And she your grandmother?"

"Aye."

"Well, I know that part better than some; born there I was, bred there, lived all me life there. What'll be the name of your grandmother?"

What'll be the name of his grandmother? "Bluett," he said. "Grandma Bluett."

The man gaped at him, opened his mouth, closed it, then brought his head down slowly as he repeated, "Ma Bluett your grandma? Aye, well, well, never go on a train I say but what you learn summit, an' that's the best I've learned this while back, Ma Bluett your grandma! Well, boy –" he put out his hand and gripped Rory's shoulder – "if you say Ma Bluett's your grandma then she's your grandma. Never contradict a stranger when he's looking you straight in the face."

The man began to button up his coat, saying, "Not far to go now, running in I should say. Glad to get something to swill this coal dust out of me throat I'll be."

A few minutes later as the train slowly puffed itself to a weary stop, Rory rose stiffly from the seat, took his canvas holdall down from the rack, then followed the man from the carriage, almost falling on his face through misjudging the depth of the step from the platform.

When he reached the man again he was talking to the porter. "My horse ready, Isaac?" he was saying, and the porter replied, "'Tis, Mr Dobell, 'tis." The man now turned and peered at Rory, saying, "How you getting to your ... your grandma's, boy?"

"I was told I'd get a slow coach, Sir."

Both the porter and the man laughed now, and the man said, "That you'll not at this time of night, neither slow, fast nor middlin'. First coach not till eight tomorrow mornin'; one goes Honiton way, an' one goes Chard way, an' your destination is dead in centre. What I'll do though I'll send one of me men over that lives by way to drop in and tell your ... your grandma you've come by, that is if he hasn't got his chores done an' left by the time I reach the farm ... She'll send a vehicle for you no doubt. Expecting you, is she?"

What should he say? "No, but she's expecting me master?" And if this woman was supposed to be his grandmother then his master would be his father, wouldn't he? So that is what he said. "No, she wasn't expectin' me but, me da ... father."

"Ohooh!" That was all the man said, but he looked at the porter, and the porter looked at him, and after a time the man said to the porter, "This is Ma Bluett's grandson, Isaac," and after a longer while the porter turned and looked at Rory and said, "You don't say! Mr Dobell. You don't say!"

"I wouldn't, Isaac, but he does; so there we have it. Well, good-night, boy; I'll do as I said."

"Good-night, Sir." He watched the man move away beyond the rim of light given off by the dangling oil lamp above the porter's head, and he asked the man,

50

"Can I wait here?"

"Aye, I suppose you can. But it's bleak outdoors; wet through and stiff you'll be in no time, mist dropping from the hills. Come along of me."

And Rory went with him. He followed the swinging lantern across a rough yard and into a room that was foggy with heat coming from an iron stove set in the middle of it, the chimney going up through the roof; the walls of the room were covered with pictures of trains, maps and sheets of paper that looked like time-tables. Along one wall stood a pallet bed. The porter now pointed to the bed saying, "I keep that there for just such a case as yours; me cottage is next door." He thumbed to the far wall. "Put yourself down and go to rest. You'll be roused quick enough when the vehicle comes."

"Ta ... thanks!" He didn't know whether to address the porter as Sir or Mister. He plumped for the Mister.

"That's all right, that's all right." Smiling broadly, the porter scratched his head and surveyed Rory as he lowered himself wearily down on to the edge of the bed, and then he muttered, "Ma Bluett's grandson! As Mr Dobell says you learn every day," and on this enigmatic remark he threw his head back and roared with laughter. And his laughter could still be heard after he had banged the door behind him leaving Rory staring at it.

. . .

It seemed to Rory that he had no sooner put his head down on the straw pillow than he was woken up again, but the face he was looking at now was not the face of the porter but that of a man with a beard and side whiskers; he was wearing a high bowler and a cloak with a double cape around his shoulders. "Who are you, boy?"

Rory gave one tight deep blink to take the sleep from his eyes. "I – I –" he looked now from the face hanging

51

over him to that of the porter at the side, and he realized that it was time for some straight explanation, so he said simply, "Mr Cornwallis sent me; he's had an accident an' couldn't come." He watched the man with the beard slowly straighten his back, take in a deep breath and then say, "Oh! that's the rights of it, is it? And you've brought a message?"

"Aye."

The man now sighed deeply, then added, "Well then, get yourself on your pins."

In answer to the authority of the voice, Rory scrambled up, grabbed for his cap, which he had thrust under the pillow, picked up the cloth bag and stood waiting while the bearded man stared at him as if he were measuring his height and strength for some feat; then of a sudden the man swung round and strode from the room.

In the station-yard, illuminated by two carriage lights, stood a one-horse carriage. "Come on then, up!" said the man abruptly.

He was no sooner seated than the horse set off at a quick trot and he had to grip on to the iron framework edging the seat to stop himself from slipping off.

He had no idea of what kind of country they were driving through, he was sure only of one thing, the horse knew the way.

They must have gone about three miles before the man spoke; then he said, "Known Cornwallis long?"

"Four, nearly five years."

"What are you to him?"

"Apprentice wheelwright."

The man turned his head swiftly and peered at him; then turned his gaze forward again, and there was no more said until the horse, suddenly dropping its trot to a walk, turned abruptly into what appeared to be a tunnel but which Rory soon realized was an avenue of tall trees. When they emerged into comparative light they were in a big yard, well paved he realized immediately, for the wheels ran smoothly across it. It was some kind of a farm.

The carriage had drawn up opposite a door which was now pulled open, and a beam of light swept across the yard. He stepped stiffly down from the carriage and the bearded man placed his hand between his shoulder blades and pushed him forward towards the light and the figure standing there. It was a woman, but Rory couldn't at first see her face because she had her back to the light, but as soon as they reached the door she stepped backwards and began speaking in a decidedly foreign tongue.

During the last two days Rory had heard all kinds of voices and although he classed them as foreign he realized they were only foreign in their dialect; but this voice was really foreign, and he couldn't put a name to it.

The man, answering in the same tongue, again pressed him forward and into the middle of the hall now. Rory's swift, first impression was that the hall was beautiful, grand. He was walking on a soft carpet, the same as mounted the stairs and glowed like a red sunset. He had a vague impression of pictures all round the hall and up the staircase wall, of gleaming furniture; then the impression was wiped from his mind for now he was looking into the face of the woman who was, he judged, Ma Bluett, for the man had just addressed her as Ma although his Ma sounded like May.

He knew that his mouth was hanging open, agape like any gormless idiot's; but he felt like a gormless idiot because he couldn't make it out. Ma Bluett was supposed to be Mr Cornwallis's mother, but the woman before him wasn't old enough; he doubted if she was as old as Mr Cornwallis. Moreover, she was a foreigner. He couldn't quite say why but he was sure in this moment that this woman could not be Mr Cornwallis's mother. And there was another thing. No wonder the porter had looked amazed when he had claimed this woman as his grandmother.

"What is your name, boy?"

He was startled by the plainness of her speech. She was no longer speaking like a foreigner; he could understand her better than he had understood anybody since he left home.

"Rory McAlister, Ma'am."

"You have, I understand, brought a message from Mr Cornwallis?"

"Yes, Ma'am."

"Give it to me."

He bit on his lip, wagged his head, then said, "I can't at the moment Missis . . . Ma'am, it's . . . it's in me shirt."

"Your shirt?"

"Aye. The Missis, she sewed it there, for safety like."

"Take your shirt off."

He looked from her to the bearded man, and the man gave a short laugh, but it wasn't unkind; then he said, "Come in here."

Rory followed him, and the woman came with him and closed the door behind her. Then, her finger pointing, she indicated that he should go and stand by the fire.

Slowly he put down the canvas bag he was still carrying; then, still slowly, he divested himself of his overcoat, coat and waistcoat; finally, pulling his shirt up out of his trousers he tugged it over his head, turned it inside out to show where the patch was, then handed it to the woman, and was surprised when she didn't take it. And he knew he wasn't imagining that her nose wrinkled slightly.

It was the man who took the shirt from him. Taking a penknife from his pocket, he carefully cut the stitches from one side of the patch, which, all things considered, Rory thought was very considerate of him, as he could quite easily have made a slit in the shirt and so come by the letter more quickly.

As the man went to unfold the letter, the woman almost snatched it from his hand, and after reading it

54

she again spoke in a foreign tongue to the man before passing the letter to him.

When he had finished reading it he looked at her and said, "He seems to lay great store by the boy." And the woman answered in English, "That doesn't alter the fact that he's still a boy."

Standing bare-chested, Rory looked from one to the other. They were talking as if he weren't there. He didn't like it; he didn't like either of them, but of the two he preferred the man. She had a sharp face, this woman, a sharp voice too; but what he thought he disliked most about her were her eyes. They were piercing eyes, yet looked colourless in this light; perhaps they were grey. She sat down now on the velvet couch, and not at all like a lady would, in spite of her voice and bearing, for she didn't spread her skirts over the seat even as the missis did, but crossed her legs and spread her arms along the back of the couch just like he himself would do against the five-barred gate that led to Rawlinson's farm.

"I suppose you're hungry?"

"Yes, Ma'am, I am."

She looked up at the man who was standing at the head of the couch and said, "Ring Jessie; tell her to get him something."

"I can see to him; Jessie needs her bed."

Yes, indeed the man was nicer than the woman; and when he picked up his shirt and threw it towards him, Rory hastily got into it and was just about to go with the man when the woman stopped him by actually lifting her foot and bringing his leg to a stop with the toe of her shoe. "How old are you?"

"Touching sixteen."

"Touching sixteen." She mimicked his voice so accurately that when he heard it he was startled. Did he sound like that? Aye, he must.

Her head strained back on to her shoulders and she looked up at the man who was standing behind the couch and once again spoke to him rapidly in the foreign tongue; but he answered in English, and in one word. "Enough," he said; and at this she rounded on him. "Enough! Enough, is it? Hawkins gone, John on his back, it just needs Ben to be laid up and then, dear brother, you'll be for the journey across the water. Think of that. Now you think of that. Unless we can get a fresh recruit or two you will have to brave the waves."

She turned her head slowly and looked at Rory, and Rory returned her stare for a moment, then looked at the man, whose head was hanging. The attitude of the big, bearded man standing as if beaten had an odd effect on him. Suddenly he felt sorry for him and he had the urge to turn on the woman and say, "You're recruiting me for nothing, missis; I've come on an errand an' once you give me whatever it is I've got to carry back I'm for home, and as fast as those trains can carry me. So you've got it." But he remembered the look on his master's face and his warning: "Say nothing except what is necessary in politeness."

A minute or so later he found himself in the kitchen; and this was as amazing in its way as the room he had just left and the hall he had first entered for it was as big as the whole wheelwright's shop if the top and bottom floors were put together, and it wasn't fitted like a kitchen with hanging meat and pans. There was little sign of cooking, yet when the man brought from the larder a platter with several slices of new bread and a big dollop of butter on it, together wih a plate holding the complete half of a chicken, he thought that even if there were no usual signs of cooking there seemed to be an abundance of food, and good at that.

He felt chary of starting to eat when the man sat opposite to him, his eyes fixed tight on him, but he was hungry. He tried to ignore the fixed stare and waded through the bread and chicken. When he was almost finished the man spoke, saying, "What'll you have to drink? Beer, milk, tea?"

"Could I have tea. please?"

"Yes, you can have tea."

He watched the man mash the tea and then place a steaming mug before him, and after drinking from it he admitted to himself he had never tasted finer; it was stronger than anything the missis had ever brewed.

"How much do you earn a week?"

He gulped on the scalding liquid before saying, "One and sixpence, an' me board." The man repeated, "One and sixpence and your board?" then shook his head, and after a moment he leant across the table, his arms folded, and said softly, "Are you ambitious?"

Ambitious? He hadn't heard the word spoken before but he knew what it meant, so he answered, "Well, I want to get on and be a wheelwright some day."

"And how much will you earn then?"

"Oh, I can get anything up to ten shillings a week, it all depends on the work I'd be doin'."

"How would you like to earn ten shillings an hour?"

"*What! Ten shillings an hour?*" Rory smiled, then shook his head derisively, and the man, his voice still low, continued as if Rory hadn't interrupted him. "And perhaps twenty pounds for a night's work."

Rory stared at the bearded face. The eyes were not like those of the woman, for they were dark brown and held a certain amount of warmth. His own face straight, he answered, "Nobody earns twenty pounds for a night's work and does it honest."

There, he had opened his mouth and said what he thought, and he shouldn't have, but the man seemed to take no objection to his remark. Instead, he said, "There's honesty and honesty, it all depends on how you look at it. You'd be doing what your master's been doing for many a year, and you consider him an honest man, don't you?"

"Oh aye, an' the best master in the world." Rory was bristling as if denying an implication in the man's words, and the man bowed his head and raised his hand as he muttered, "All right, all right; we won't go into that."

Again the man was staring at him and this time he surprised him with the question, "Do you go to church?"

"Sometimes; feast days like harvest time and such, but not Sunday school. They mostly go to Sunday school to learn their letters, I know me letters; me da learned me, he's a great reader is me da."

"You can read then?" The man's eyebrows had moved up.

"Aye, I can write an' all."

"That's interesting, very interesting, I know some men, craftsmen, who can't even sign their names."

"The master can, the master's a good writer."

Rory now saw a change come over the bearded face. It was like a ripple of laughter, derisive laughter, yet the offence it might have held was taken away by his words when he said, "Oh yes, your master can write; we know that, God help him."

It was now the turn of Rory's eyebrows to move upwards. The man was pitying his master. He saw no reason why anybody should pity Mr Cornwallis.

Rory watched the man scrape his chair back on the stone floor and recognized a change in his voice when he said, "Well, are you ready?"

Whilst the man took a lamp from a side table and lit it, Rory wiped his mouth with the back of his hand and picked up his belongings from a chair; then he was following the man again, upstairs now, but not the stairs that led from the hall. These were narrower stairs, but nevertheless they had a carpet on them. The landing that they gave on to was long and had five doors. The man opened the second one on the left hand side and said, "You'll find what you want in there," then, pointing along the corridor to the end door, he added, "That's the water closet."

Water closet! A water closet inside the house! Would he never stop being surprised in this place? Again he wanted to open his mouth and say, "I'm not using any

59

water closet inside, it's not decent. The missis doesn't even allow chamber pots except when you're bad in bed." But he said nothing.

When he was bidden, "Good-night," he said, "Good-night," and added "Sir," and went in and closed the door.

He carried the lamp to a table by the side of the single bed. The room was furnished in grand style. He sighed deeply. It was all beyond him; perhaps things wouldn't be so confused in the morning. What he wanted was sleep, a good night's sleep. Hastily he got out of his clothes, then shivered as he slipped in between the questionable luxury of sheets, and his last thought before sleep overtook him was, why should that fella be sorry for the master?

Chapter Four

"Sleep till you're buried, you will, then wake up'n find yourself dead."

'W–what! Where am ... who?' Rory dragged himself up out of a deep sleep and on to his elbow and stared at the laughing face looking down at him. It was a plump face, a pretty face, and young. He drew back from it, saying, "Who are you? What do you want?"

"To gettin' you out of bed, that's what I want." When the girl's hand took the top quilt and threw it back he grabbed the remaining bedclothes around him and, sitting up, cried at her, "You leave me be! I can get up without your help, thank you very much."

The girl, about to make a laughing remark, was checked by a harsh voice from the door, crying, "Tilda!"

They both stared now at the old white-capped woman glaring at them, and the young girl, her face dropping into sullen lines, cried back at the woman, but in a muted tone, "Am just doin' what I'm told."

"Come out of it!"

Rory watched the girl walk sulkily out of the room and bang the door after her; then the old woman's voice came to him, saying, "You scut you! that's what you are, a scut."

"Scut yerself, you Jessie. 'Twas the mistress who told me. 'Go up,' she said; 'get him out of bed if you have to pull him.' That's what she said. Oh you! old you are, cranky."

Before the voices had faded into the distance Rory was out of bed and into his trousers, and within five minutes he was washed and fully dressed and walking cautiously down the corridor.

When he reached the bottom of the stairs he again saw the girl and his face turned scarlet; but she was her usual merry self. "Mistress is in the long room," she said. "She's waitin' for you."

When he came within arm's length of her she put out her hand and pushed him in the shoulder, saying, "What be frit of? Face is red as a cock's comb. Don't be frit, yarm too big to have yer backside tanned."

Well, of all the cheeky monkeys! For two pins he'd skelp her lug for her; he would that.

"Go on." She actually pushed him through the door, and he found himself in the hall once again and knew he hadn't imagined that the place was full of colour, for now in the morning light it appeared like a great painted picture of reds, greens and golds.

"The door under the arch." She dared to push him again. "Knock first, else you'll get your head knocked off."

He managed to bestow on her a withering glance before he walked across the hall and knocked on the oak door that fitted into the rounded arch.

"Come in."

The woman was sitting at a desk at the far end of the room and she didn't speak or raise her head until he was standing before her, and then she looked up at him and smiled; and he was mystified, because her face looked pleasant.

"Sit down, Rory."

She must have got his name from the letter. He sat down, his eyes fixed tight on her.

"Well now –" she leant back in her chair, her elbows

on the arms, her finger tips tapping each other. With her head on one side she said in the most pleasant manner, "You're only going to be here for a short time so we must see that you enjoy it, mustn't we? Do you like the country?"

"Yes, Ma'am."

"Have you ever lived on a farm?"

"No, Ma'am."

"Then you must go round the farm this morning, and later, take a drive. I have need to send someone to Upottery; you'll enjoy the drive and you can visit Yarcombe on the way. You'll never see finer country than around here."

"Yes, Ma'am."

"And when you come back you must tell me what you think about it."

"Yes, Ma'am."

"Have you ever thought about leaving the North of England and looking for your fortune elsewhere?"

"No, Ma'am. I ... I like the North, an' ... an' me people are there."

"Yes, yes of course." She moved her head once, and now she asked, "Mr Cornwallis, do you think he is seriously hurt?"

"Very, Ma'am, I should say. It may be that he'll never move again."

"Oh!" She turned her head away without taking her eyes from his face.

"I understand you can write."

"Yes, Ma'am."

"How well can you write?"

"I can write me name, Ma'am, and words, an' reckon money."

"Really!" There was surprise in her voice; then bending forward she picked up a sheet of paper that was placed to the right of her hand and said. "Show me how well you can write. Write your name; what is your full name?"

"Rodney Thomas McAlister, Ma'am."

"Rodney Thomas McAlister. Oh, we want a nice clean space for that name, don't we?" She folded the sheet of paper over several times and when she handed it to him there was left a clean oblong strip that would take his name. When she nodded towards the feather quill pen he took it out of the inkwell and wrote in a round clear hand, upstrokes thin, down strokes thick, Rodney Thomas McAlister. When he handed it to her she stared at it for a moment; then, looking into his face again, she smiled and said, "Yes, indeed you can write."

Sitting straight up in her chair again, the paper with his name on held in her hand, her tone took on a briskness as she said, "It being Sunday you will not get the right impression of the work that goes on on the farm, but nevertheless you can wander around. Go now to the kitchen and Jessie will give you some breakfast. My brother should be leaving for Upottery around one o'clock. You won't have your dinner until you return so I'd advise you to eat well at breakfast.

He was standing now. "Thank you, Ma'am."

She smiled at him again and he turned from her and walked down the long length of the room knowing that her eyes were upon him.

In the hall he looked about him; he guessed that the passage that led from the backstairs would also lead to the kitchen. He supposed that was where the cheeky monkey had been coming from when he had last seen her.

After crossing the hall he hesitated between two doors, then went through the one at his left. No sooner was he on the other side than he knew it was the wrong door, for here he was in a small hall with an open door at the end of it leading on to what looked like a terrace.

Well, he reasoned, he had only to walk round the terrace and he would come to the kitchen door, wouldn't he?

In walking along two sides of the terrace he had

passed a number of windows but no kitchen door, and it was as he turned a corner yet again that the voices came to him. He recognized them immediately; one was that of the woman who had just been talking to him, and the other was the voice of the bearded man, her brother, and it was he who was saying, "None of your tricks, May; he's different, it could mean trouble."

"Don't be ridiculous, Alex; a boy earning one and sixpence a week, different, huh! Don't be ridiculous."

"I tell you I feel he's different, he's got spirit."

"So had his master."

"It was a dirty trick to play on the lad."

"I may not use it; if he's wise I won't have to use it. I've told him he's going with you today; I didn't tell him I was supplying a companion for him besides yourself. We'll see what interests him most, Tilda's charm or the scenery."

"You're too clever, May." The statement was full of bitterness, and was followed by a silence during which Rory stood, his head cocked to one side, his fingers nervously tapping his lower lip. That woman; he knew he hadn't liked her from the start. But what trick had she played on him? She had done nothing to him when he was in that room. But what had he done? Nothing; just answered her questions and showed her that he could write ... *write!* His eyes sprang wide; he had written his name on a piece of paper. He could see her now folding it. There had been writing on the paper, and she had covered it up ... Aw – he shook his head at himself – he was being daft, imagining things. But the man had just said she had played a dirty trick on him. He couldn't really get to the bottom of it, but one thing he did know, she wasn't a good woman – planning to send that cheeky monkey along of him this afternoon in order that she could take his fancy.

He turned now and tip-toed back along the terrace and into the hall. He wished he was home; by lad! he wished he was home. They could keep the scenery, and their farm, an' the beautiful house ... an' that cheeky monkey an' all, they could keep the lot. Give him the wheelwright's shop and his bed under the eaves an' Mrs Cornwallis baking in the kitchen, an' Lily with her kind face and sweet voice ... And the master ... the master who was an honest man. The master who travelled hundreds of miles every two years or so to visit his mother, and the mother was Ma Bluett ... He mustn't start suspecting the master, that was the last thing he must do. But it was all very odd, aye, an' that was putting it mildly.

. . .

For the past half-hour he had sat crushed up against the 'cheeky monkey', who was sitting between him and the bearded man on the seat of the high go-cart; and his term for her became more appropriate with the journey for she chatted not only to him, but also to her master. He supposed the man was her master, seeing that his sister was her mistress. Yet this much he had gathered: the bearded man might be tall and stern-looking, but he didn't wear the breeches in the household; in some ways he seemed no better than a servant; it was the woman, with her beautiful face and oddly big hands like those of a man, who wore the breeches.

He had to admit that the country they were driving through was bonny, but it wasn't his type of country, too soft like, as he put it to himself.

When they drove into a tiny village with a grey stone church on one side and a few cottages on the other, it was raining heavily and the man said to him, "Get down and go with Tilda; I'll pick you up on the way back."

When the girl went to push past his knees, saying, "Well, get you down," he remained tightly fixed in his seat and glared from her to the man, saying, "Where's she goin'?"

"To her mother's. Go on, get down; I won't be long,

not more than an hour or so."

He got down, and watched the cart roll away along the rough road, and Tilda, laughing from under her hood, said, "Come on, run, we'll be soaked else. 'Tis just along the lane."

He didn't move but looked about him, and his eyes became fixed on the church. Then looking at her again, he said, "You can go along on your own, I'll wait in the church."

"What!" Her nose wrinkled, her lips parted, showing a large mouthful of square white teeth. "You daft or summat? That there's mouldy, smelly, and as dank as the grave. Come on, you fat head." She made a grab at him.

"Fat head!" He was bristling. "Who's a fat head? Don't you call me names. An' get your hands off me an' get yourself away."

Her face straight now, she looked at him in bewilderment. She couldn't understand him; no boy of his age had ever before said no to her. He was a queer one, odd.

"You mean you're not a' comin'? ... Mam makes a good tea Sundays."

"Well you eat it," he barked ungraciously. Then turning from her, he went down the sloping path and followed it round the side of a square towered building until he came to the church door. Turning the heavy handle, he pushed against the black oak and went inside, and knew immediately that she had been right about one thing anyway. It was smelly, and as cold as the grave.

Hesitantly he walked to the centre aisle. Lor! he had seen stables cleaner than this. It looked as if the whole place had never been used for years. But a snuffed candle to the left of him told him that somebody had been there and quite recently.

He began to walk around, spelling out names inscribed in stone which meant nothing to him. He was going up the one step to look at the choir stalls which

68

appeared very old, when he turned swiftly around on the sound of the door opening.

When the bearded man beckoned to him he went hastily down the aisle. He had never thought he'd be glad to see him so soon again, but he was. He even made a joke saying, "That hour or so's flown."

The bearded man gave a thin smile as he said, "I didn't have to go as far as Upottery for I met Ben just outside the village. This here is Ben Bachelor." He nodded towards the thick-set man, then said, "This is the boy, Rory."

The man, Ben, was staring at him, looking him up and down. Then he nodded his head and said, "Aye, Rory. Well now, can you sail?"

"Sail? You mean sail a boat?"

"Well, you wouldn't sail a farm cart, would you, boy?" and the man laughed, causing Rory to blush slightly and retort swiftly, "Nor would you gallop a train for that matter; but as I've never been in a boat I know nowt of sailin'."

The man, Ben, now gave a deep chuckle as he said, "Well, by the spirit of you, boy, you could manage a galley." He turned and looked at the bearded man and said briefly, "It could be worse."

"That's what I said." The bearded man nodded; then looking at Rory and making a motion with his hands and his expression looking quite friendly, he commented, "You were looking round. Fine old church."

"Come on, Alex." The other man had turned away and pulled the door open, adding, "Get you on your hobby horse of churches and we'll be doing a tour. As for me, this place always gives me the colly-wobbles."

Outside, standing close to the wall away from the heavy rain, the bearded man who Rory now understood was called Alex, asked of Ben, "How are you going to get back? There's not room in the trap unless you hang on and sprint."

"I'll sprint without the aid of the trap," answered

Ben, "I'll cut over the fields, an' I'd like to bet I'll be there afore you." He was walking backwards as he spoke; then his step was checked by Alex Bluett saying quietly, "Don't stop at Compton's, mind, she wants you sober."

"Who's going to stop at Compton's?" Ben laughed back. "'Twould be no use anyway, it being Sunday. Drunk as a lord on Saturday, sober as a judge on Sunday, canned as a Canon on Monday, you're forgetting the days of the week, Alex." The man turned away now and ran between the leaning headstones in the little graveyard that surrounded the church, and when he came to the hedge he leapt it with the agility of a deer and was gone from their sight. Alex Bluett, with a shake of his head, looked at Rory and said, "Come on, let's get out of this. We'll go and pick up Tilda; though she won't like it, she'll hardly have got going with her gossip yet."

He smiled slyly at Rory, but Rory did not give him an answering smile, for his mind was becoming more and more troubled. Why had that man Ben asked him if he could sail a boat? He had never hidden the fact that he had no love for the sea. Perhaps it was because he had never even been able to swim, never had time to try for that matter. Where was he expected to sail a boat to?

By! he wished he was out of this, he did that.

. . .

Ben Bachelor was as good as his word. When they drove into the farmyard in the fading light there he was, a pipe in his mouth and grinning at them. He greeted Alex Bluett, saying, "What did I tell you? Been here these past ten minutes."

This was another thing that Rory couldn't understand: this Ben Bachelor was dressed like a working man, yet he spoke to the master of the place like an equal. He wished he could fathom it all out.

His eyes were now drawn to the far corner of the yard where an elderly farm servant was making a hand step for Miss Bluett to dismount from a horse. In this moment two things registered with him: first, the servants on the farm were nearly all old men, and secondly, Miss Bluett was wearing breeches just like a man. She had a sort of skirt over the top of them which came to her knees; it had a split up the front but didn't hide the fact that she was dressed in trousers.

She came briskly across the yard now and, to his embarrassment, it was himself whom she addressed first, saying, "Apart from the weather, what do you think of our countryside?"

"It could be bonny."

"Huh! it is bonny. And did you enjoy Mother Young's tea?"

"Wouldn't come in with me, Mistress." It was Tilda speaking, her face and tone petulant now. "Not be good enough for foreign numskulls, we're not!"

Miss Bluett looked after the flouncing figure going towards the kitchen, then turning a sidelong glance on her brother as she moved towards the front of the house, she said on a laughing note and half under her breath, "That's one avenue closed. And the countryside has little attraction either I should say. Have you any better ideas?"

"Shut up!"

This admonition from her brother turned her about and, her face stiff with sudden anger, she glared at him, but restrained herself from making a retort. Instead she hurried on and, if she did not flounce like Tilda, her feelings were expressed in the straightness of her back and the set of her head.

Alex Bluett now turned to Rory. "Go to the kitchen," he said. "Make a good meal —" he paused. "Have you an extra coat?"

"Yes, Sir."

"Then I'd advise you to put it on. Come into the hall within say —" he turned towards Ben Bachelor now, and Ben said, "Half-an-hour or so."

71

"Make it half-an-hour," said Alex Bluett.

'Yes, Sir."

"That door there, the second one, that's the kitchen."

Again Rory said, "Yes, Sir." Then without hurry he walked towards the kitchen, tapped on the door and entered the room.

As if she had been expecting him the old servant said, "Come and sit down, boy. Give your coat here and I'll dry it off. Not that it'll be much use; wet again it'll be before it's been on two minutes. There now." She took the coat from him, smiled a thin toothless smile at him, then pointed to the table and the well stocked plate, saying, "Get it down you, boy; you may need it before the night's out."

As he sat down at the table he wondered grimly what she meant: he'd need it afore the night was out? There was one thing sure, they weren't going to get him on doing something that he shouldn't be doing. He was going to ask what it was all about afore he set off anywhere. Yet he must remember what the master had said, say nothing except in politeness. Aw dear, he couldn't even enjoy this food because of the state his mind was in, and it was good food. The ham was sweet and melted in the mouth, and the sausage was mostly pork, not three quarters bread and barley.

At one point he stopped chewing and muttered, "Where'll I be bound for in a boat?" and Jessie said, "What you say, boy?" and to this he answered, "Nothing. Nothing . . ."

While he was still eating, Jessie left the kitchen and when she returned she said, "Hurry up and finish boy. Get into your coat, and go and wait in the hall. Stand near the foot of the stairs, don't roam."

A few minutes later he was standing near the foot of the stairs, and when a door opened at the far side of the hall he heard Miss Bluett say sharply, "Why didn't you tell me this before, Ben?"

"Didn't want to trouble you."

"Trouble me!" The voice was scornful now, then went on, "Two strangers walking the cliffs between Seaton and Sidmouth and you didn't want to trouble me!"

"Well, could have been anybody. Still could."

"Oh, you're a thick head, Ben." Her voice was scornful. "It's God's wonder we've got this far without trouble."

"Well we have, haven't we?" There was a sound of laughter in Ben's voice. "Anyway," he said, "whether I be a thick head, dolt, or clean lunatic, I'm the only one you can trust to do the trip, that's a fact. Now, isn't it?"

Rory saw Ben in the doorway now, and he watched him turn his head towards the room again as Miss Bluett's voice said softly, "Be careful, Ben, I don't like the way things have gone. Hawkins going off like that, God knows where. Cornwallis laid up, and it may be for life."

"Why should you worry?"

Rory raised his eyebrows at Ben Bachelor's tone, which was heavy with scorn. And he was amazed when Ben continued, "Your tin trunk's mighty heavy by now, May, and you've got enough of the other to deck out a dozen dowagers . . ."

"Be quiet!"

There was a silence in the hall. The clock chimed the quarter of the hour to five. Rory looked down at his feet while he waited; then there came the sound of a door banging and the next moment two pairs of feet came within his vision and he looked up and saw Mr Bluett and Ben Bachelor. He hadn't realized that Mr Bluett had been present during the conversation he had overheard, for not once had he heard him speak. And neither of them spoke to him now but went towards the main door, and on a motion from Ben's head he followed them.

Silently he climbed into the trap that was waiting in the yard with lamps lit and a man holding the horse's head.

Chapter Five

It was still raining heavily and there was a wind with it. It wasn't like the icy blasts that swept the fells but was soft and clogging, a steamy wind as if it were coming from the spout of a hot kettle ...

He could not judge the time accurately but he guessed it was about half-an-hour later when the trap stopped and Ben, jumping down, said to him, "Come on, boy."

When he was on the ground he stood by Ben's side looking up through the flickering light from the rain-washed lamps at Alex Bluett who, bending over, now peered at Ben and said, "Go careful, Ben." There followed a pause before he added, "I get worried, but then why should I, you know the ropes, nobody better. Tuesday morning first light then, I'll be in the usual place. Touch wood –" he touched the side of the trap before ending, "I've only once had to go up to the point, I wouldn't want to do it again, and not for you, Ben."

"Don't you worry, Alex, old fish swim deep, you won't have to go up to the point. Good-bye now, see you Tuesday, early light."

"Early light it is. Good-bye, Ben, and good luck."

They shook hands firmly as Ben answered, "I've always had that, if nothing else and I always will; a man must have something ... Come, boy." There was a tug on Rory's arm, and like someone in a daze he now felt himself being guided over what appeared to be hummocks of sand and saltwort.

It was black dark, literally, for he couldn't see his hand before his face.

The terrain changed, and now he knew they were going over rocks, for his feet were slipping all over the place, and he was just saved from going flat on his face by Ben jerking him upwards and his voice coming through the darkness, hissing softly, "Steady! Steady!" Then reassuringly he said, "Not much farther, keep close."

"Stand just where you are," whispered Ben now. "Don't move, I'll be back in a few minutes."

The following seconds seemed like minutes, and the minutes took on the length of hours. As Rory stood in the rain-washed blackness, fear that he hadn't experienced before started to gallop through him. What if Ben didn't come back and he was in some kind of cove and the tide came up?

"Steady now! steady now!" Ben took his hand and his voice was a reassuring whisper. "There's nothing to get worried about. Come on." The next minute when the cold water rushed into his boots he gulped and cried out, "Aw! Aw! ... Aw, man!"

"Ssh! keep your voice down." Ben's tone was a growl now. "It's only salt water, do you no harm. Been wet half me life, never had a cold ... Here we are; climb aboard."

Rory felt the flat of Ben's hand on his buttocks shoving him upwards, and he tumbled over the side of the boat, then over some kind of seat, and landed in a huddle, with his hands and knees this time in water. And now another fear sprang at him; he was in a boat that had water in it.

At this point he tried to speak, to make some protest, ask where he was going, ask what it was all about, but Ben's hand was now on his collar pulling him upwards, whispering hoarsely, "Come on out of it, along here. Feel this seat; lift your feet, that's it, around the cabin. Now sit yourself down here, close to me. Put your hand on mine . . . This is the tiller. Get the feel of it, because you'll likely become acquainted with it long before the night's out. Go on, grip it, it's not going to bite you. That's the way. Now hold it there, just like that until I tell you to move it to port or starboard."

"W-what!" The word came as a croak from Rory's throat.

"All right, we'll make it left or right for the time being; but for the moment just keep it like that, just like that."

Rory, realizing he was in sole charge of the tiller now, began to sweat, and the sweat joined the rivulets of rain running down his face even while his whole body shivered. He heard oars grating in the rowlocks; then the boat began to move, bobbing up and down, like a dumpling in broth, as he put it to himself. After a while he thought, in panic, I'll . . . I'll be sick.

Then the motion changed. One minute the boat seemed to be going straight down into the water and the next his stomach indicated that he was going to do a back somersault.

"Mister . . . Mister Bach . . . Bachelor." His voice was high above the wind, and the next second so heavy was the grip on his shoulder that he thought Ben Bachelor was going to lift him bodily and throw him over the side.

And now Ben was hissing hoarsely in his ear, "Keep your voice down, you thundering idiot! Don't you know it could carry over the cliffs in this wind . . . Oh my God!" Ben now grabbed the tiller as it swung madly from side to side; then, the boat on course again and his voice less harsh, he said, "Sorry, boy; but you've got to learn. Somebody could have taken that for a cry of help and would get the boat out, and then where would we be? . . . Aw, I'm sorry."

Rory felt a gentle punch against his chest, then a firm

grip on his arm as his body fell towards the side of the boat, and after a moment, during which Ben held him tightly against his side, he said, "You don't see things clear yet, boy, you don't understand the half of it. Give me time and I'll put you right. Now we're through the channel and clear of the rocks the wind's in our favour; I'll set the sail and then it should be easier going. The rain'll stop shortly; it always comes in with the new moon. Now if I could do this journey in a full moon, why that would be just dandy. Pity. Pity. But there it is. Well now, from here on do as I bid you. If I say a little to the left push it to the left like this; if I say to the right, like this, and for straight ahead level with your knee." He now groped at Rory's leg and, moving it, said, "Keep it just there."

In the period immediately following, during which the boat was running under its small sail, Rory's mind was wiped clean of every thought but one; he was sick. And he kept telling himself this: "I feel sick. Oh dearie God, I feel sick." And when the voice, out of the darkness, came to him saying, "A little to the left ... right hand over ... straighten her out," he obeyed it automatically, until in a moment of desperation, when his stomach heaved up into his mouth, he let go of the tiller and, turning, leant over the boat's side and gave up to the sea the fine meal of sweet bacon and sausage.

"You'll feel better now. Here, straighten up and take a drink of this."

Rory thrust the bottle away from his mouth, for he never wanted to eat or drink again as long as he lived. But he felt helpless to protest against Ben pouring the liquid down his throat. It burned in its passage and set his stomach on fire. Coughing and spluttering, he bent over double. Oh dear me. He had never known such depths of misery in his life. If only he could die, finish it ... When the bottle was again thrust into his mouth he fought off the hand holding it, but not before he had once more taken a long drink.

"There now, that'll settle you. Come on, you can doss down in the cabin. I can manage for the next few hours or so; as long as Mistress Moon keeps to her pattern and doesn't give us a squall just for good measure. Careful now, over the seat ... Don't try to stand up, there's no head room in here. There's the bunk and blankets; and they're dry. Careful now, steady."

Under Ben's guiding hand Rory tumbled into the bunk and never was he so thankful in his life to lie down flat. His whole body was warm now with a kind of glow, and his stomach had stopped trying to escape through his mouth; nevertheless, as he felt himself falling into sleep he hoped he'd never wake up again, for if he did he knew he would have to take that tiller; and go through all this again, and it was too much to ask of anybody. Even for Mr Cornwallis's sake he couldn't do it.

. . .

He woke of his own accord, and for a moment couldn't remember where he was until the motion of his bed told him. But the motion now was gentle, nothing like it had been when he had lain down. It was still black dark in the little cabin but to the right, by the foot of the bunk, the darkness seemed to lighten.

After a time of lying in gently rocking comfort he slowly dragged himself out of the bunk and went towards the door, and as he was about to speak, Ben Bachelor's voice came to him, saying, "Well, you've had a good stretch, boy."

"Aye." He could make out the dark bulk of Ben beyond the billowing sail, and he stumbled his way to the stern and, flopping down beside him, he said, "I feel I've been asleep all night."

"And you have."

"Really! you let me sleep all night?"

"No need to wake you; it's been a fine night and a fair wind. It's only in the getting out from the beach and going in that I need help; except in a calm, and then it's a matter of using the oars all the way, otherwise I could take her across these waters with me eyes closed. Feel better?"

"Aye ... yes, I feel much better." He was very surprised that he could say this for he didn't feel sick anymore. "What time do you think it is?"

"Round six o'clock."

"Six o'clock in the morning?"

"Well, it isn't six o'clock in the evening, boy, that's for sure; another hour and the sun'll be coming up. But we want to get in before that."

"Where we going?" For the first time Rory pointedly asked the question that had been filling his mind, and was given the answer immediately.

"Jersey."

"*Jersey! Jersey?* That's an island, isn't it?"

"It's an island, boy."

"What are you going to do there?"

"Oh, you'll know soon enough; don't get too curious. Keep your eyes open and your mouth shut, that's the best policy."

Practically the same advice that his master had given him; but it was difficult advice to take when you were being thrust into the middle of something that didn't seem altogether above board. When business was above board you didn't travel by night, especially on the water. Were they going to smuggle something? Oh no. He dismissed the idea. Mr Cornwallis would have no hand in shady business like smuggling ever; he'd stake his life on that. Then what was it all about?

"Ah, the wind's veering a bit."

Rory could feel no difference himself but Ben's sniffing nose seemed to be acting as a weather vane for, "North now," he said; "and if she gets round to North East we must watch it. It could blow us towards Rouge Nez and Grosnez Points; but, once beyond Grosnez, and if she keeps North she'll blow us kindly down to Bouley Bay."

"Is that where we're bound for this Bowerly Bay?"

"Yes, boy, that's where we're bound for, Bowerly Bay."

Ben's mimicking of his pronounciation made him press his lips together and turn his head away.

. . .

It was an hour later when, with excitement in his voice, Ben called to Rory, saying, "Stand up, boy, and look there!" And Rory stood up and, following Ben's pointing finger, saw rising out of the sea great patches of colour, purples, browns, reds and golds, and as he looked the sun, rising behind him, spread over the colours like the light from a thousand lamps and brought them alive and glowing; glowing with such an intensity that Rory found his breath catching in his throat.

"Bouley Bay."

Rory did not turn and look at Ben, but kept his eyes on the great cliffs rising from the sea and, gently shading, as if with a golden hand, the bay itself. He was still gazing fascinated at the sight when the picture slewed away to the right of him and he turned quickly and looked at Ben and asked, "You're not going in there then?"

"Not in the actual bay, boy. See that jut of rock sticking out. There's a pier there; it's for the fishermen, the oyster catchers. They might take us for poachers, and that wouldn't do at all, might set the gun battery on us." Ben chuckled.

"Gun battery!"

Ben laughed outright now. "Don't look so scared boy. But at the same time don't think the beautiful island is peopled by saints who live in peace; it's not eighty years since they had to defend themselves against Highlanders who landed on that very beach.

"Highlands from England, I mean Scotland?"

"Aye, Scottish Highlanders from England. Oh, they've had their troubles here; for the size of it the

80

island's had more trouble than a monkey in a vat of molasses ... But now get to the tiller or we'll be on the rocks, and May won't like that, will she?''

May? He was referring to Miss Bluett as May! As he gripped the tiller Rory looked closely at the man who was dressed like a servant but didn't act like one; anyway, certainly not towards the mistress of St Helier House.

"Now do exactly as I say, do you hear?" Ben's voice had changed, its tone was a command now. "Keep her dead straight until I say hard a'port, left, you know left, then take her over as far as she'll go, understand?''

Rory did not answer but nodded his head, and now Ben almost barked at him, "Speak, boy! Answer aye or nay; you can't hear a nod of the head in the dark."

It was on the tip of Rory's tongue to say, "But it isn't dark now,'' but he realized there was sense in what Ben was saying, and so somewhat grudgingly he said, "Aye."

"Hard over left, sharp."

As the boat swung half-way round, Rory glanced in apprehension at the rock jutting above the water. They had missed it by no more than a foot or so. Lord! His wits became sharp; his eyes were fixed on Ben, who with an oar in his hand was pushing it against the rocks as if he were punting.

"Keep her sailing. A bit to the left ... That's it, just like that ... Now over to starboard ... right! right, boy! Take her gently now, hold her there."

Rory realized that he was sweating. The boat was now beating swiftly through a passage lined with rocks; then of a sudden he felt it being dragged to a slow stop and, looking over the side, saw that they were in shallow water with golden sand not three feet from the water line.

"There now." Rory looked up into Ben's grinning face. "We've made it. Not bad, boy, not bad, seeing it's the first time you've had your feet wet. Think you'll like the sea?"

"*No!* No. I can't ever see meself liking it."

Ben gave a deep chuckle, then tousled Rory's hair and, his voice changing, he said, "You're a good boy." Then as he turned away he muttered, "It's a pity."

What was a pity in being a good lad . . . boy?

"Benny! Benny!"

They both turned and saw a figure springing lightly down the heather-clad rock that sloped steeply up from the small sandy bay. Ben, his face alight, called back, "Hi there, Lawrence!" Jumping out of the boat, he ran forward to meet the man, and they shook hands warmly. They both came towards the boat now and Ben, his voice gay, shouted, "Come on, boy, unless you're going to sail her back on your own. Jump in, the water's warmer here."

When Rory dropped into the water, which he had to admit was considerably warmer than that into which he had stepped last night, but nevertheless had a chill about it, the small thick-set man, who stood at the water's lapping edge, did what everyone else had done since he had left his own part of the country, he looked him up and down. Then he turned to Ben and asked, "John? What's happened to John?"

"Hurt his back, Lawrence. Bad, I understand. This is his boy, not his son, but a good boy, he mentioned him to me on his last trip. His name's Rory."

"Well, if John says he's good, then he's good. Welcome Rory." The man held out his hand, and Rory took it and liked what he saw. The man could have been taken for a native of Northumberland, that is if he hadn't opened his mouth, for although he spoke English he was definitely a foreigner by the way he pronounced his words.

"Come on, come on," he said now; "Let's get this up –" he looked towards the boat – "and then make for home."

After they had beached the boat Ben said, "How did you know we were here? I saw no one on the pier."

"Oh, I was gathering vraic with Jean and Frederick

around the next bay, I recognized her." He thumbed back to the boat.

"Jean and Frederick?" Ben's voice was quiet as he repeated the names, and Lawrence put in quickly on a laugh, "Oh, don't worry about them, they'd put false bottoms in their breeches." At this both men laughed while Rory looked from one to the other; then turning to him, Ben said, "It's a joke. They used to build ships on the island with false bottoms for smuggling. It's a joke you see."

"Oh aye." Rory nodded, but didn't smile, he couldn't see any joke.

Then they began to climb a rocky slope so steep that he needed all his wind to keep going. The two men were well ahead of him and when eventually he reached the top they looked at him and laughed, but didn't immediately move on; and he stood to the side of them gaping in amazement down on to the bay lying cupped between two great rocky hills. The one he had just climbed, and stretching away both to the right and to the left of him, were filigreed rocks edging sandy bays which ran into the blue sea, and everywhere he looked there was colour, great patches of colour, not so bright as it had looked with the first rays of the sun on it, but bright, warmly bright now.

When the man Lawrence laughed and spoke rapidly in French Ben turned to Rory and said, "He says you look mesmerized."

"It's very bonny."

"Ver-ray bon-ney," repeated Lawrence; "I agree it is, ver-ray, ver-ray bon-ney. Aren't you ver-ray hungry?"

"Aye, yes, I am a bit." Here was another one making game. They should listen to themselves.

"That'll soon be put right." Ben dug him in the ribs with his elbow. "Wait till you see your breakfast."

. . .

It was an hour later when Rory finished his breakfast and thought, I'll never feel fuller. He had got through a bowl of porridge and thick cream, a plate of fried belly pork and crisp potatoes, and four slices of bread cut from the biggest loaf he had ever seen.

He sat back now and looked to where Ben and Lawrence were in deep conversation, then he tried to keep his gaze away from the very old woman who sat staring, unblinking at him. She was Lawrence's mother, he understood; she wore a black wool dress and a black bonnet with a white full underneath; she was toothless and kept champing her lips.

There were two other women in the kitchen: one was Lawrence's wife; the other was his daughter. These two women, unlike the old one, looked merry and had chatted all the time they were serving the meal, and to Rory's discomfort they had laughed heartily when Ben described his amazement on seeing the cows tethered like goats and with blankets over their backs; which had been nothing, he said, to when he had seen the ten feet tall cabbages and goggled until his eyeballs had nearly dropped out.

In a way, he liked Ben, but he'd like him better if he didn't take the rise out of him.

The old woman now joined in the men's muted conversation and Rory sat back in his chair and looked about him. His eyes travelled upwards. There was a wooden rack like a double clothes horse hanging above the table, and on it were laid loaves and jars and bottles, and herbs hung in bunches from the bottom of it.

Next to a tall grandfather clock at the end of the room a blackbird twitted shrilly as it hopped about its cage. He didn't like that, not to see a blackbird caged. Years ago when he was small he had been in a house where they had a linnet in a cage, and he had sneaked up and let it out. But the poor thing had nearly dashed itself to bits in its freedom, for it was blind. It had had its eyes poked out in order that it should sing better. He remembered he had cried that night and was sick over the bed.

The kitchen wasn't like any farm-house kitchen he had ever seen, nor for that matter was the house or farm. The cabbages they grew might be whoppers but the fields they grew them in were nothing more than patches compared to those back home. Yet everything about the little farm looked solid, he had never seen a house with walls so thick. He looked towards where the big open fireplace, with its angled spit was let into the wall and was admiring the fancy ironwork on the spit support when he almost bolted out of the chair as the old grandmother suddenly gripped his arm and spoke to him rapidly in her own tongue.

"It's all right," said Ben laughing; "she's only asking how old you are, and if you have a mother and father, brothers and sisters."

Rory nodded at Ben now, saying, "Aye, I've got a mother and father and five brothers and sisters, an' I'll ... be sixteen this time next week."

It was Lawrence who interpreted this to the old woman, and she now nodded brightly at Rory and to his further embarrassment touched his cheeks as she again spoke to him.

"She says you've got a fine face, you'll make a fine man," said Ben, still laughing. Then he added, "No need to bow your head, boy; you know how you look yourself. Well now –" Ben pushed his chair back from the table and, addressing Lawrence said, "I'm for bed Lawrence; I'm dead on me feet and there's another long night afore us. I'll leave everything to you then?"

"Yes, Ben, as usual leave everything to me, it's all in order. It's a long time since we had so much blue baccy ..."

As soon as Lawrence had used these last two words he turned quickly and looked towards Rory; then Ben said quietly, "It's all right, he knows nothing as yet, but he'll have to because May has recruited him."

"So soon?" Lawrence was staring at Ben, and Ben said, "So soon."

"She is not good, that May."

"Ssh! ssh! Ben turned away, then added, "Come boy; you slept I know, but it's ten to one you've got a wakeful night before you, the weather doesn't look too easy, so get all the rest you can." He turned to Lawrence now, saying, "The same room, Lawrence?" and Lawrence replied, "The same room, Ben."

Rory followed Ben along a stone passage up a narrow steep winding staircase. The bedrooms opened one into the other and the room they finally entered was small and from the middle of the ceiling the roof sloped steeply down, which told Rory this was the end of the house. A bed with a winged headboard stood in the middle of the room.

"There." Ben pointed. "Get your clothes off and tumble in."

Rory had the urge to say "I'm not a bit tired, I'd like to go out and look round," for he had come to the conclusion that this island was indeed bonny and he'd like to see more of it; but he guessed rightly that he wouldn't be allowed to go out on his own. You didn't come sneaking into a cove then flaunt yourself to all the inhabitants. He wished he knew what they were talking about half the time; there was something very fishy about this whole business. Yet those people downstairs were nice, he could swear they were nice; everyone he had met since he had left the North had been nice, except that Miss Bluett and her brother. But even he on his own was all right, and Ben had evidently liked him, and called him Alex ... But what was this blue baccy? And why was it so important that they had come for it by night? Well, he was going to find out, and now, this minute.

It was as if Ben had read his thoughts, and he actually started as Ben, climbing on to the high bed, said, "Now don't start firing questions at me because they'll be like

87

peas hitting an iron plate, they'll just come back at you. I'm dead beat, boy, so climb yourself in and take my advice and sleep, for if you don't, this time tonight you'll wish you had. Hear that wind, it's a gentle north-easter now but it'll veer and be a raging one by tonight, or I'm much mistaken, so get tucked in and sleep.''

Grimly Rory climbed up into the bed and into a wallow of feathers, which comfort, he told himself, under other circumstances would have knocked him clean off to sleep, but not now, for he wasn't tired.

He lay with his hands behind his head, his mind going round and round the problem – blue baccy. What was it? A special kind of baccy that had been discovered? No. No; that was daft, all kinds of baccy were brown or black, blue baccy ... blue baccy ... He didn't remember drifting off to sleep.

. . .

He awoke slowly. He stretched and turned over on to his face then blew some feather down from his lips, and, his head hanging half over the edge of the bed, he became conscious of being wonderfully rested and feeling that he wanted to stay like this for ever. There was a murmur of voices going on somewhere but it did not disturb him in any way; in fact it began to act as a lullaby might and send him once more off into sleep ... When his head came up with a jerk and his eyes opened wide he knew something in the murmuring had disturbed him.

He looked about him. It was still daylight, high daylight; the sun was coming at a slant through the little window in the sloping roof. What time would it be, one o'clock or so? He turned his head now and looked across the bed. Ben wasn't there. He hadn't heard him get up, but now it was his voice he knew he was listening to coming from the other room.

He looked towards the open door not far from the foot of the bed; then he hitched himself towards the middle of the bed. Now he could see into the room. Two figures were bending over something on a small table and he knew instinctively that whatever they had come to the island for was on that table. The thing that was called by the two words, the words that had brought him wide awake out of sleep, was on that table.

Slowly he lowered his legs over the side of the bed and slipped to the floor; then he moved towards the open doorway. Before he reached it, however, he stopped when he heard Lawrence's voice say, "It was a job to get them all into the two, and it was a pity that it had to be broken, it was so bonny." He gave a little laugh and Ben's voice answered, "It would have been broken in any case, wouldn't it? This is the biggest yet. Surely this'll satisfy her."

Again there came the laugh from Lawrence, but with no vestige of merriment in it now as he said, "Nothing will satisfy May. She's got this in her blood now; and with it power, power over so many. It was all supposed to be for when Philip comes back, to make it up to him, but the way she's going, and the greed of her, if she's not careful she mayn't be here to meet him when he comes back. And that would be irony wouldn't it?"

"Irony indeed, Lawrence. And I've been in a similar mind over the affair meself many a time of late."

"Where's this lot for, do you know?"

"John's way. It's safer; that's why she sent for him."

"Poor John! he must have been in a sweat. If he hadn't sent the boy she wouldn't have believed he was ill, and he'd have been lying there, wondering ... wondering. Do you think she would have carried out her threat?"

There was a pause before Ben spoke; then, his voice slow, he said, "I haven't a doubt of it, Lawrence. And he would have been transported to start his twenty-five years about the time Philip was coming back."

"Aye, it's hard to think, Ben, she's of my own blood,

although distant. And this boy; he'll have to be let into the know."

"Yes, that's true. But it'll have to be broken gently to him, for he's got a stubborn streak in him. And the pity of it is, he's an honest lad."

"You say she's got him fixed?"

"Yes, she's got him fixed, in any case she's got him fixed by carrying the baccy. But should he try to get out of that, there's his name at the bottom of a paper."

"Oh, not that old trick."

"Aye; she still works it and to some effect, where she thinks they're gullible and won't fight back. But I've told her she's picked the wrong one in this lad, for what I've seen of him he's got spirit, and he'll fight her in his own way, not knowing that he's bound to lose in the end ... Do you know how she got her latest contact in Plymouth?"

"No."

"Huh! talk about a mind; she should have been a general, with the manoeuvres she gets up to. You'll never guess what her latest was. She staged a shanghaiing of a fellow for the navy; then, of course, Alex came to the rescue and brought him to the house and she hid him for two or three days before sending him off to live in Ireland – it was the only place she hadn't a contact."

"Dear, dear God! that woman."

Rory was saying the same words to himself. That woman. She was a fiend, but if she thought she had got him into her clutches she was making a mistake. He wasn't having any of their monkey business and getting himself transported. By no, lad! he'd tell them so right away. And at this he walked forward into the room, startling the two men for a moment; then Ben laughed and said, "You've slept, boy, haven't you?"

Rory glared at him. "Never mind how I slept; I didn't sleep long enough, that's evident, I've heard what you've just been sayin'. And let me tell you I'm havin' none of it,

I'm not in any of your smugglin' rackets."

The two men exchanged glances before Lawrence said, "Boy, whether you like it or not you're in. But I know how you feel, we both know how you feel. We're not bad men . . ."

"Well, you're not good 'uns either of you."

"What do you think of your master, John Cornwallis?"

"You leave me master out of this, me master's the best man walkin'. Now you leave him out . . ." He paused, then looked swiftly from one to the other, and Ben said, "Yes, yes, now you're thinking, boy, aren't you? Your master's a good man, yet he sends you right down to Devon to May Bluett's house, doesn't he?"

"By what I can gather he's been tricked an'all."

Again the men exchanged glances; and now it was the Frenchman who answered, saying, "Strangely, he's about the only one of us who hasn't been tricked in some way or another; if justice was working correctly your master would be in Australia this minute along with May's brother, my half-cousin, Philip."

His mouth slightly agape, Rory stared at the man. He knew he was speaking the truth, yet he still couldn't believe it. His master was a God-fearing man, he had lived in the North all his life. No, no, he hadn't. He remembered Peter Tollett talking about the time he left his father's shop and went to sea. Three years he was away and when he came back his father was on his death-bed and so he stayed and took up the business from there. Then his mother married again, a man she had known in her early years, and went to live in Liverpool. Yes, it was Liverpool, he remembered. But they must have moved to the West Country for it was to the West Country that his master had come to visit his mother. His ma? Miss Bluett? Ma or May Bluett? He couldn't get this straight at all. There were so many things he couldn't get straight he didn't know which end of him was up. The master's words came to him: "You

91

hold my life in your hands, boy."

He would do anything for his master, he owed him so much. But did he owe him this much, which meant getting himself mixed up with a gang of smugglers, because that's what they were? They said they weren't bad men, and somehow they weren't, but nevertheless they were smuggling and there was a penalty on smuggling. Yet he knew that all kinds of men, in all kinds of classes, went in for smuggling; parsons and priests, doctors and lawyers, had been known to dabble in it; but somehow he had the strange feeling that this wasn't ordinary smuggling.

He moved his bare feet on the wooden floor, straightened his shoulders, jerked his chin upwards, then said, "What's blue baccy?"

The two men didn't move, they didn't exchange glances, they just stared at him.

There started inside him a tremor that he would have liked to disassociate from fear, but it was saying, "They could murder me an' nobody would know, because nobody knows I'm here except them two in that mad house over there." The beautiful house had, for him, now turned into a mad house, ruled over by a mad woman. His sweat was beginning to dampen his hair when Ben lifted his arm and with pointing finger said, "That's blue baccy, boy."

Slowly he turned his gaze and looked down on the table where lay two small cart-wheels of baccy. It was what was known as twist baccy; it was brown and about an inch in depth and each cart-wheel did not measure more than three inches across. His whole face screwed up in bewilderment. Blue baccy; it was the ordinariest baccy he had ever seen. He had seen hard twists and flat black baccy like the sailors chewed; he had seen shag baccy and the big rolls of baccy from which the shopkeepers sliced off whatever a customer wanted, a pennorth, two pennorth according to your means; there were fancy baccies put in boxes – these had certain scents to them he was told; but what he was looking at now was a little flat cart-wheel of cheap baccy. He turned slowly and looked from one man to the other and Ben said quietly, "That's blue baccy, boy."

"Why do you call it blue?"

Ben's mouth opened, his face went into a twisted smile and he said, "Ah-ha! well now! that can wait. What do you think Lawrence?" and Lawrence, his face too taking on a lighter expression, said, "Yes, Ben, that can wait. Let us eat; enough is enough. Go on, boy, get your clothes on then come down to a meal, and some cider. That'll soften the questions in you."

The Frenchman now pushed him hard on the shoulder and after a moment, while he looked from one to the other, he turned away, and as if still in a deep dream he went into the other room and slowly got into his clothes. *Blue baccy!* He felt utterly deflated and slightly silly.

Chapter Six

Rory considered the meal to be like a party you would have at a wedding, or a harvest supper. The table was laden with all kinds of food: a leg of roast pork, cold ham, meat pies, and fruit pies; cakes with burnt brown sugar on the top and tarts covered in cream; besides which there was cider, great jars of it.

Everyone was seated at the table, all helping each other to this or that food, and all aiming at once to help him, that is with the exception of the grandmother, who from time to time stared at him blankly and addressed him in her foreign tongue, and as the meal went on became more and more querulous. At one point, her hand gesticulating backwards and forwards across the table, she covered him with a spate of words until her son, Lawrence, said, "Take no heed, she's in her cider mood. Always like this with too much cider in her." Turning to his mother, he now said in English, "Enough old lady, now! Enough! We know that all the boards in the island are not spread like this, but there is bread for all, so don't keep harping back to forty-seven."

He turned to Rory and said, "There was an uprising of the workers a few years ago. Bread was very dear; they attacked the mill and were only quelled when the

94

troops were called out ... but –'' he spread his hands wide – ''that is all past, now we have enough and plenty for all who come. And they do come –'' he wagged his finger at Rory. ''From all over the world they seek refuge here, Poles, Russians, Hungarians, Italians, aye, and even Frenchmen fleeing from old Nap. Aye, they all come here. Do you know, boy, this is but the world in miniature; everything happens here, wrecks, cholera. Yes, and not forgettin' the creation of colleges. We're having a college built, boy. And Louis Blanc's here. Do you know about Louis Blanc? No, no, you wouldn't, boy. Great Frenchman Louis Blanc, the workers' friend, Louis Blanc, but France has no use for him. Here's to Louis Blanc.'' He raised his mug of cider and took a long draught; then he cried, ''And here's to Ben, drink to Ben.'' And they all drank to Ben. Rory too; he kept sipping at his cider, but it got no less for they would insist on refilling his mug. He didn't know how much he had drunk; he only knew that he liked them all very much, even the grannie who kept shouting at him when she must know he couldn't understand a word she said.

''Drink to Rory. Rory O'Mory. Drink to Rory.''

''Me name's McAlister.''

''His name's McAlister.'' They were choking with their laughter.

Oh they were funny. He was enjoying himself as he had never done before. And the food was wonderful, marvellous; he had never tasted anything like it; he was chock-a-block with cream. Vaguely, at the back of his mind he thought of his family. What would they not give to sit at a table like this. But the thought brought him no pain, as it would have done at another time. He was so warm inside, his head was light, and he felt quite merry. An unusual feeling for him.

After a few more sips of cider he heard himself laughing, and they were all pointing at him and lying half over the table in their mirth. Had he said something funny? No, he hadn't opened his mouth. Perhaps he looked funny when he laughed. . . . Well, he felt happy.

When he could eat no more he sat back and gazed happily at the activity about him. He watched the table being cleared, then bottles of wine being placed on it, together with three large rolls of tobacco and a foot long plain wooden box.

Lawrence turned to him and, pointing to the box, said, "Snuff, enough snuff to sneeze a town. Highlander's snuff, you know." He dug Rory in the shoulder. "When you come again I'll take you into the town and show you the statue of the big Highlander. Outside the shop of baccy, he stands, the big Highlander, taking snuff . . . I like you, boy," Lawrence's face came close to Rory's. "You tell John I like you. You won't forget, will you?"

Rory shook his head, still smiling.

"And tickle Scape's whiskers for me for luck, boy, will you? Oh aye, tickle Scape's whiskers for me."

Into Rory's befuddled mind there struggled the question of why this man, hundreds of miles away from the wheelwright's shop and across the sea, should know about Scape. But then he gave himself the laughing answer. Scape was a joke; likely Mr Cornwallis had made them laugh about Scape's escapades and her running away over the fells every time she got loose and making straight for the Inn at Gateshead. Everybody laughed at Scape's liking for beer. Peter Tollett was known to bring her a drop now and then, although Mr Cornwallis didn't like it. Yes, that must be how this Frenchman knew about the goat . . .

. . .

Rory's memory of the farewells he made to the Lesauteur family was vague. Only one or two things stood out: the young woman, who was called Elizabeth, kissing him on both cheeks and him trying to push her away, which caused everybody to roar again with

96

laughter; and then Lawrence standing in the passageway somewhat apart from the others and patting Ben's chest as he said, "Safe journey, blue baccy. Yes indeed, for all our sakes, a safe journey," and Ben taking Lawrence's hand and saying, "Never fear, Lawrence, never fear."

Then Lawrence had asked, "How's your head?"

"Clear as a bell, Lawrence. You know that I never go over the third pint; and a cider has never been brewed that could knock me out in three."

Rory recollected vaguely a strange young man coming on the scene at the last moment and that his name was Raoul, and he was the husband of Elizabeth and was a militia man. He was also vaguely aware that it was Raoul who led him through the dark lanes and down the steep cliff side to the shore, while Ben and Lawrence followed behind. And he recalled, while on the beach, Lawrence whispering thickly, "The boy'll be no help to you, Ben; Raoul'll push you through the rocks."

He himself was then pushed into the boat, and he stammered, "I . . . I'm all r—right, Ben . . . Tiller. I can take the . . . tiller."

"You stay quiet and don't move. Sit there. Now sit there." Ben's hands pushed him down and on to the bottom of the boat near the entrance to the small cabin and, his voice no longer merry now, he hissed at him, "Stay put! Now do you hear? Stay put until I tell you to move."

Rory stayed put. The boat began to move. He heard the soft good-byes beween Lawrence and Ben. Then he felt the boat heave and some time later Ben's voice, saying, "Good enough Raoul, I'm all right now. Good-bye."

"Good-bye, Ben. Good trip. Good luck."

Everything was soft, muted. The motion of the boat was gentle; the night was black; and he was suddenly very, very tired. He laid his head in the crook of his arm and, knowing little of the danger he was in and caring less, he went to sleep.

. . .

"Wake up, boy. Wake up, you've had enough. Come on."

The hand on his shoulder pulled him into a sitting position. Through slit eyes he peered down into the cabin where a lantern was burning low. "Come on. Come down here and drink this."

When he went to obey the order his head seemed to bounce upwards off his shoulders. When it settled again the pain of it made him shudder. He covered his eyes with his hand as Ben's voice came to him, saying, "Yes, cleft in two, that's what it feels like. Come on down and drink this; this'll put you right."

When he turned on to his hands and knees he was aware that the back of his clothes were soaking wet. He had been lying in water, and he was shivering like a leaf. He took the big mug into his trembling hands and his face screwed up still further as he drank the bitter black cold coffee.

Not until he drained the mug could he speak, and then he said apologetically, "I'm sorry, but ... but I'm not used to cider."

"That's pretty clear, boy."

"How long have I been asleep?"

"Four hours or so."

"Oh." He shook his head. "I'm sorry I wasn't able to help you get the boat out."

"Oh, that's all right. We were in luck, the weather was kind ... Feel better?"

"Me head's achin' ... splittin'."

"That'll clear in a short while when you get the wind through you. Speaking of wind, if the squall doesn't come and she keeps like this we should be in well before sunrise tomorrow morning, around six I should say, for she's going straight and sweet."

He now leant over and peered at a small compass set in a brass case, then said, "If the wind holds good I'll have a nap myself; that is, come early morning. Never trust the wind till after midnight, boy. Speaking of trust –" he now picked up the brown coffee mug and poured himself out some more coffee before asking, "Do you trust me?"

Rory was taken aback by the straight question; then because he was built as he was he gave the straight answer, "Not very much," he said.

"Good enough. If you had said otherwise I wouldn't have believed you ... What did you hear this morning from your bed?"

Rory's mind was not quite clear yet, and he had to think hard for a moment. Then he said, "Enough to know that I've been tricked; that she, Miss Bluett back there, got me to sign me name to something which will give her a hold over me. At least she thinks it will. But it won't, you know, 'cos I'll fight her."

"I like your spirit, boy, but believe me when I say, those words have been said before but to no avail."

Rory felt that thread of fear again going through him; and now he asked quietly, "Who is she, anyway?"

"Well, I could say she is Miss May Bluett who was born on a little scrap of a farm not ten miles from the house she lives in now, and she has two brothers, one you've met, Alex, and a younger one called Philip. But when I've said that, that's only telling you about one Miss Bluett; I know half-a-dozen."

"Well I've only met one of her an' I think she's awful."

"Yes, she's awful, boy ... and wonderful. It's just how you look at her."

"What's all this got to do with my master? How did she trick him?"

"It's funny you using the word trick, but as Lawrence said to you a while back, John was the only one she didn't actually trick, not intentionally anyway, he tricked himself. It's an old story and if it doesn't happen every day it happens pretty often. By the way, did you like the house, St Helier?"

"Aye, I thought it was bonny, but ... but I don't want to see it again."

"But you thought it was bonny, and it is bonny. That's what May Bluett thought when she saw it first as a young lass. But she thought the master of it was bonnier still. Conway they called him, Henry Charles Montague Conway. He was as fancy looking as his name. All the women thought him pretty; May thought him beautiful, and she decided to have him. And when May decides to have anything she gets it. She rode like a man – she has always ridden like a man – and she rode full tilt for him, for he was a big prize; he had looks, a fine house, which, by the way, May coveted from the day she first saw its gables, and he was also supposed to be rich. So she won the race and snared him. Aye, that's the word, snared. Like a hunting dog with a rabbit, she snared him. Well, about the same time her brother Philip was making good headway with a bonny piece from as far away as Dawlish. Bella Nesbitt was her name. And one day Bella Nesbitt and Henry Charles Montague Conway met. Now you can perhaps guess the rest, eh?"

Rory shook his head and, his eyes wide, he kept them fixed on Ben, and for a moment he forgot he was rocking in the middle of the ocean in a tiny lamp-lit cabin in which it was impossible to stand upright. Then Ben went on, "No? Well, you being sixteen I thought it would have been evident. Anyway, a fortnight before May was due to marry Henry Conway, what does he do but run off with Bella. Can you imagine, boy, the scandal that caused? It ricocheted for miles around, from the Blackdown Hills to Bridport, from Glastonbury to Exmouth. People laughed behind their hands, for they knew that the hunter had lost her quarry; and a hunter May certainly was and she didn't care who knew it. To say that she was bitter is putting it mild, and there's no knowing what she might have done if her favourite brother, Philip, hadn't taken a hand. Now Philip was a well set-up fellow himself, proud and a bit blustering, but he had one weakness, drink, and because of his hurt he went on a spree that took him as far away as Plymouth, and there in a bar he meets a man ... Now can you guess the man's name?"

Again Rory shook his head for he had no idea.

"Well, his name was John Cornwallis, and they both of them got stinking drunk together ..."

"That's a lie. Mr Cornwallis doesn't drink; never has ..."

"Boy, I know that John doesn't drink now, he won't even touch cider, but he went to sea for some time and it's very rarely you find a dry sailor. At one time John could stack it away like a vat in a brewery."

There was such a ring of truth about this statement that it silenced Rory, and after a moment Ben went on, "When they finally reached Philip's farm, which was a few miles beyond Upottery towards Culmstock, they were still drunk, for they had been drinking at every inn along the road. And late that very night Philip, accompanied by John went to St Helier House, and there called on Conway to come out and fight. Conway came out, and Philip fought him while the young sailor man –" Ben now nodded at Rory – "who is your master, fought off the servants with a swinging stave, and all the while the young wife and the female servants stood screaming inside the house.

"Two days later when Conway died, they routed Philip out and put him in jail, but they couldn't lay hands on the bearded sailor. Nobody knew his name, or where he had come from, and it was strange, but nobody for miles around appeared to have seen him. The sympathy, you see, was all with Philip and whoever this man was who had helped him to take vengeance on Conway. Such is human nature that a few weeks previously they had been laughing behind their hands at him and his sister for both having been baulked in the chase.

"I said nobody knew about the bearded sailor; but

there was one who knew, May. She kept him hidden at the farm for weeks, and then, clean shaven and dressed like a tramp of the road, he made his way to his people's home in the North. I didn't know him then; I didn't know him until some years later when we made our first trip across these waters. You see, May never does anything for nothing; she had the sailor in the hollow of her hand. Her brother had escaped the gallows and been sentenced to twenty-five years deportation, and the very fact that Bella Nesbitt, or Mrs Conway as she was, had died of grief three months after her husband was killed did not satisfy May. She made a vow. She would have the house that she should have been mistress of, and she would keep it in style, and, his term on Botany Bay finished, Philip would become master of it and the farm.

"After Bella Conway died it was discovered that her husband had not been the rich man that people supposed. The house and farm were put up for sale and were bought by a foreigner. Well, he was a foreigner in that he came from yon side of London Town. But he only stayed for a little more than a year, for strange things were always happening around. His cattle got sick, his barn took alight, the fish died in the brook. He said there was a curse on the place and he sold it for much less than he had paid for it ... And who bought it? May. Where did she get the money from? A cousin on the island had died, it was said, and left her his money; quite a good sum of money, it was said. Another cousin came over from the island to back this up. His name was Lawrence Lesauteur. Do you follow me?"

Rory paused before moving his head slowly downwards and saying, "Aye, the ... the money was from smuggling?"

"Yes, smuggling, but ... but not ordinary smuggling. There's not a lot to be made out of that." Ben looked down at the floor of the cabin and clapped his heels twice against the dirty wood under which lay the bottles, the box of snuff and the baccy. "Baccy and brandy bring small money really, unless done in a big way. A false hold full might bring you in a nice bit, but amounts like this . . ." he again tapped his heel – "Who would risk their necks for it? Nobody but an idiot. No; May went in for the big prizes; big prizes gathered from small bulk, like so." He now put his hand flat on his chest. "As you heard Lawrence say back there, the refugees flood into the island from all parts of the world. They bring with them only what they can carry, their most treasured possessions, and they very often have to sell them for next to nothing. Well, that's how the blue baccy started. But when you get too many in one business the profits are thin and you have to look elsewhere, and May looked elsewhere. It's one kind of risk bringing over refugee's stock, but it's altogether another when you act as transport for stuff that the constables of half-a-dozen countries are looking for."

When Rory's hand went slowly up to his mouth Ben said, "I'm telling you this for a purpose, because I think I can break it to you better, and more kindly, than she would. You see, as John was partner to the unhappy Philip, you're partner to me. At least that's how May sees it. And so whether you like it or not, boy, she has you trapped."

"She can't! She won't! I'll tell the truth."

"Well, if it came to the point and you did tell the truth, I'm telling you now, and this is the truth also, that if she had to pay for her deeds she would see that you paid too. She's a woman nearing her fifties. She hasn't all that long left, but you, boy, are just starting life, and she would see . . . Now I'm telling you in deep earnest, she would see that you spent most of that life where her brother is now, in a penal settlement in Australia. And what is more, if she's caught, John's caught too. Sick bed he may be on, but that wouldn't soften her. She said these very words to me herself a few minutes before we left the house, for I had said to her your very words.

What if he won't stand for it and gives you away? 'Let him,' she said; 'and he'll give his master away at the same time. I'd make that clear to him right at the beginning'.''

Rory's lower lip trembled slightly as he said, ''She's a wicked woman, a real wicked woman.''

''Yes, I suppose she is.''

''You suppose she is!'' Rory leant across the narrow table now. ''There's no suppose about it, she is. You ... you seem to take her side.''

''No, no, I don't take her side, boy. But you're young and you've got a lot to learn about life and people and their strange ways.''

''You do; you do take her side ... Why?''

''That's a good question, boy, a good question. Would you understand it if I said it's because I ... I love her?''

Rory's eyes stretched wide while Ben nodded at him. ''You see, I was brought up alongside of her, and since I was your age, oh, and for a while before, I thought that one day I'd marry her. She was then a wee bit above me in position, but that didn't matter. I danced with her at the barn dances, I held her hand walking through the fields.'' Ben turned his face away now and looked through the small open door into the black night. ''Since the day she heard that Conway had gone off with Bella she's never touched a man's hand, not even Alex's, her brother's. But then she thinks little of Alex. Poor Alex; he has no spunk, he's like a wild rabbit caged in a backyard.''

He now turned and looked at Rory and, tapping his chest, said, ''Even when I hand her the blue baccy she doesn't touch my hand.''

There was a depth of sadness in the statement, and as Rory peered at the stocky, stubbly-faced man sitting opposite he felt a sadness well in him too and thought that, against all reason, he liked this man. He looked at Ben's hand still placed on his chest and he asked the vital question, ''Why,'' he said, ''do you call it blue baccy?''

"Ha! the answer to that is simple really. Her name's Bluett. When I first met up with Lawrence he used to call the small packages Bluett baccy; then it became shortened to ... blue baccy. When a message was sent out to me, or to John, or to any of the others, and the words blue baccy were in it, we knew what it meant ... and the danger it implied."

"Has ... has she a hold on you?"

For the first time during the conversation Ben laughed. It was an ironic, self-denigrating laugh. "No, boy; she hasn't a thing on me. She treats me like a dog, a faithful dog, and like a faithful dog I haven't the sense to transfer my loyalty, because you know, she's lonely, she's a lonely woman. So I stick around and run when she whistles. It'll be like that to the end."

Rory said softly, "I'm sorry."

"Thank you, boy. It's the first time anyone has said they were sorry for me."

"But ... but Ben."

"Yes, boy?"

Rory now swallowed and wiped the sweat from around his face, for in spite of his wet clothes he was sweating, and his voice held a distinct tremor as he said, "I'm ... I'm a bit frightened."

"Don't worry about that, boy; I'm nearly always frightened."

"But ... but you don't understand. If anything happened to me I ... I don't know what would become of me family. I'm, I'm the main support."

"A family?" The query was high, rather amused. But Rory's answer was grave as he said, "Me da, he's dying with consumption; an' me ma's sick an' all, but that's from lack of good food. And then there's five others; they ... they depend mostly on me wage and what the missis gives me to take back in me spare time."

Ben's hand came across the table now and gripped Rory's as he said, "Well, that's one worry you needn't have anymore for, give her her due, she pays well. You'll

105

have more money than you know what to do with, boy. Do you know something? I've got over five hundred pounds stacked away under the hearth stone." He spread his hands wide now. "But what's five hundred pounds; I can only use money now and again when I go on a visit to my uncle in London." Now he chuckled deeply as he ended, "And me uncle moves about. He's been in every public house in that City, and that's some travel I can tell you." He laughed ruefully. "But it's the only way I can spend a bit of the money, for if I started splashing it round about here the people would become suspicious. You know what people are."

Ben now rose to his feet, saying, "But come now, we've had enough talk, we'd better get outside and see the weather." He bent and took Rory's hand. "Don't worry, boy; you've got to take risks in all walks of life, and in all walks you meet men, good, bad, and indifferent. And sometimes you find the bad ones not half as bad as the good ones, and the indifferent ones so torn between the two you can't tell t'other from which."

As he gave Rory his familiar jocular punch his words were recalling to Rory those of Mr Cornwallis on the same subject. And a question sprang to his mind and he asked, "What happens to the blue baccy, when she gets it?"

"Oh, that," Ben's eyebrows moved upwards. "John takes it back with him and the scapegoat does the rest."

"Scapegoat! you mean our goat, Scape?"

"Yes, your goat Scape. Why do you think she was trained to like beer?"

"What's the goat got to do with the blue baccy?"

"A great deal. When she's let out she makes straight for a certain inn, hell for leather I'm told. And who's going to stop a goat on your fells, and feel under her chin, especially at night?"

"But ... but why do they send the goat if Mr Cornwallis has carried the blue baccy all that way. Why can't he finish the job and take it to the Inn?"

"Aw, boy, you know little about the Excise men, they haunt the inns as stealthily as ghosts, and what you are forgetting is that John is known as a sober man, he would not frequent an inn. Furthermore there are only two contacts in any one place and in the Inn at Gateshead there is the owner and a Swede, the Swede is the go-between for the far countries like Norway. But come, let's get on deck. I've done enough talking for the present."

. . .

It was about one o'clock in the morning when Ben, handing the tiller to Rory, said, "All you've got to do is to keep her straight. If you get worried give me a shout. I'll sleep two hours, no more; I can wake up to order. You're not afraid, are you, to be left on your own?"

It was dark, so Rory's expression did not give his feelings away, and he made his voice steady as he replied, "No, I'll be all right."

But no sooner had Ben left him than a wave of fear overtook him, and it wasn't only because he was in a boat steering it blindly and without knowledge, or that the darkness around him was as black as if he had been buried in the bowels of the earth, or because the swell of the sea had complete control of his innards, pushing them up and thrusting them down at will; but it was the future that terrified him.

If he were to defy that woman she would, as Ben had said, see that he was put away, and retribution would fall on his master.

When he thought of his master, parts of his mind attacked the loyalty he bore him. He would have sworn the master had never done a bad thing in his life. He hadn't really. Yet hadn't he been drunk? But lots of men got drunk, and that didn't mean they were bad. But there was the big thing his master had done; he had carried the blue baccy and used poor old Scape. To his mind that was a dirty trick. Poor old Scape.

Would somebody say in years to come that *you* were bad because you were forced to carry the blue baccy? It was as if a voice were coming across the water, accusing him.

The master had said, "There's nobody black inside, boy, and nobody white."

One good thing would come out of it anyway, he consoled himself, his folks would eat. Ben said she was generous. But he didn't want them to eat through her generosity, for he hated her already.

He leaned back and peered up into the blackness. Was there a God who helped people? He had never prayed much; his mind wandered when in church, he got bored, but he knew now that if ever he needed to pray it was during the next few hours before the boat grounded on to that beach. But how could prayer get him out of this fix? There was no opening that he could see; that devil of a woman had shut every door. It was no good. Anyway, he thought, he was like his father; he hadn't any room for people who ran to God just when they were in a tight corner. Making a convenience of Him, his father had said. But if he could only be shown a way out, given a chance.

The tiller jerking violently in his hand, cut off his thinking, and when the sail flapped wildly and the boat swung into the wind he yelled, "Ben! Ben!"

A minute passed before he heard Ben shouting "It's all right. It's all right," as he tackled the sail. Then a long space before he took the tiller from his hand, saying, "That sleep was short and sweet. But it happens like this; we're in for a squall, and some rough seas."

That was all he needed to know. They were going into a rough sea. If he were seasick again, well . . .

During the next hour the wind rose and the rain started suddenly, and stopped suddenly. "Spiteful! she is, the night. Spiteful!" shouted Ben at one time.

Then as the boat swung round and Rory almost went

over her side, Ben yelled at him in an angry tone, "Don't be such a damn fool, boy! Keep your grip on something. Have you no sense?"

From then onwards Rory had sense. Whatever he had to move he did so with one hand grasping the gunwale, and all the while thinking that the night would never end.

His teeth chattering, cold and shivering, Rory asked, "What . . . what time is it, do you think?"

"Close on five, boy," said Ben kindly. "Not much longer now. If it were daylight we'd see the coast plain.

"Once –" he laughed shortly – "the light came up and I saw the coast plain, but where do you think I was? Almost opposite Start Point. Couldn't tell to this day how I went that far wrong. More than once I've had to land at Sidmouth, and in the other direction along the coast towards Weymouth, but I was never as far out as Start Point. I think that was one of the nights I went over my third, and not with cider either. I've learned since; we all learn, boy."

It was as Ben said, they would be in about six o'clock. The wind was still high, the rain still coming in squalls. Ben sat by the tiller, his eyes straining ahead, for although it was still dark the deep blackness was lifting. He was in the middle of repeating, "Not long now," when the words trailed away and, putting out his hand and gripping Rory's knee, he said, "Look yonder, boy, away to the left. What do you see?"

Rory turned his head and looked to the left, and for a moment saw nothing. Then, piercing the darkness, he made out a thin speck of light. It disappeared, then came again; disappeared, then came again.

"My God!" muttered Ben.

"What is it?"

"Trouble."

"Is . . . is that a signal from the bay?"

"No, boy, not from the bay, but it's a signal all right. And it's coming from near Beer Head. It's only happened once before. In all my runs it's only happened once before."

"What does it mean?"

"Well, you'd better know, boy, it means that somebody is on to us. How that's come about I don't know ... Yet I do; and I pooh-poohed it. The two strangers walking the cliffs ... Well, I've beaten them before, I can do it again. Now listen, boy, and listen carefully." His voice was gruff and sharp. "From now on, everything I say jump to it as if your life depended on it, for it does. Do you hear me, boy, it surely does. One wrong move and we might reach Australia without May's help, the both of us. You understand?"

Rory said nothing, but he understood and he trembled with his understanding.

"Now then." Ben loosened the main sheet into his hand; then, taking the tiller, swung the boat into the wind and began tacking, the bows headed first one way and then the other, and before long Rory became tired with folding up his body to keep it clear of the swinging boom.

He guessed now that they were heading towards the light that was piercing the darkness in a series of three flashes. At one stage he asked breathlessly, "If ... if you hadn't seen the light, what then?"

"Well, then we would have sailed straight into a trap."

"But ... but how do they know what time to expect you?"

"Oh, they know. Within an hour or so they know. It's a matter of the tides. On some full tides you would never get near the shore, for they sweep to the cliffs."

When Rory next saw the light he thought to himself, I can't count now, but he knew that he had counted aright when he heard a sound like a groan coming from Ben. "How many flashes did you see there, boy?" Ben asked now.

"I thought it was four."

"It was four."

"Is that worse?"

"Yes, yes, it's worse." Ben did not speak for some time. He seemed to be concentrating on the sheet and the tiller; then of a sudden he said to Rory, "Here, catch hold for a minute!" And when Rory had taken the tiller Ben swiftly undid his top coat, then his under jacket and waistcoat. From inside the shirt he now pulled out a small calico bag and, having opened it, he drew out one of the little circles of tobacco. "You know what I'm going to do, boy?" he said.

"No," said Rory briefly.

"Feel that." He pushed a circle of tobacco into Rory's hand. "What is it?"

"It's one of them cart-wheels of baccy, blue baccy." Rory laid harsh emphasis on the words.

"Blue baccy indeed. Blue baccy," repeated Ben. "And I'm going to trust you with it. Now listen, boy. We may have to split up and run for it. If they get wind of us, they'll likely chase one or the other; 'tisn't likely there'll be enough of them to divide up. If you should be cornered and you haven't time, get rid of it. Here's a trick. Open your coats."

Rory did as he was bid; then he felt Ben's hand fumbling in his shirt and he shivered when the coil of tobacco was pushed against his flesh.

"You've got a belt on, haven't you?"

"Aye, you know I have."

"Well, should you be running and they're on you, loosen your belt, give yourself a shake and it'll drop down your trouser leg. Take your stockings off."

"Me stockings?"

"Aye, boy." Ben's voice was harsh with impatience. "Your stockings, it could drop on top of them and be caught up."

Rory unlaced his boots and took off his stockings, and he almost groaned aloud as he put his bare feet back into the cold wet boots.

"Now listen further. We're going to land where it's pretty rocky. The boat'll have to take its chance, and so will we, for we'll be up to our necks in water until we reach the cliff ... Can you swim?"

"No." The word was short but it held a long tremor.

"Well, I'll stay close to you until we reach the cliff. It goes almost straight up there, but there are a number of rough paths. You'll go one way and I'll go the other; the light'll be breaking, you'll be able to see. It's covered with gorse and low scrub, there's plenty to hang on to, and it's riddled with hidey holes. Before it's full light find one and stay there until you reckon it's safe to make your way to the top of the cliff. Up there, there's a field, and beyond it a narrow road. Don't ask your way of anybody, for you won't know whether it's friend or foe you're talking to. Look for the signpost; that'll lead you to Axminster, then on to the house. If I get away the other road – and I will – I'll come looking for you. Now you've got all that?"

"Aye," said Rory, but with uncertainty.

"Good! well now, brace yourself, boy ..."

They were running before the wind when Ben gave the warning. His voice grim, he said, "When I say jump, jump. You'll likely go straight down to the bottom for I can't pinpoint exactly where we are in this light, but we're not far off the shore. Of that I'm certain. The only thing is, if you value your life don't cry out. Do you hear me?"

Rory had no voice with which to answer. He knew that once he dropped into the water he would drown; he hadn't the faintest idea how to swim. For a flashing moment he had a strange experience. He could have sworn he saw Lily smiling at him, and her face wasn't plain, it was bonny. And she had young Sammy with her. Of all the family he thought he loved Sammy the best.

The picture vanished as Ben's voice hissed in his ear, "Over with you!" Then he was pushed.

112

Down, down, down, he went into the cold black water, and he knew that this was death.

Excruciating pain dragged him upwards. It was Ben's hand grabbing his hair. His head rose above the waves and he began to thrash out with his arms and legs. Just as he was about to sink once more he felt Ben's hand under his chin; and then his body seemed to slide over Ben's, and it was as if he were resting on it.

An eternity later, his feet touched something firm and his head came up out of the water. Then with Ben's arm about his back, he was stumbling towards the shore.

When he felt the water receding and knew he was dragging his feet up a hard slope all he desired was to throw himself flat and rest, but Ben's arm kept him going.

It was as he raised his head and peered through the early morning mist towards the towering cliffs in front of him that the shot rang out and for a moment he felt Ben's arm drop away from him, but before he fell to his knees the arm was around him again; and now they were running in step like two children in a three-legged race.

As they scrambled up the cliff path, the desperation of the situation seemed to clear his mind and he used his hands frantically to pull himself upwards and away from the shouts coming now from below them. When a voice rang clear through the air shouting "Stop! in the name of the law!" and something sharp hit the rock face ahead of them, he couldn't believe it. He wouldn't believe that they were being fired on. A silly voice inside his head kept saying that he was Rory McAlister, apprentice wheelwright to Mr Cornwallis; he had never done anything really wrong in his life except scrumping apples; there was that once he had stolen a hen because the bairns had had no food for two days, not even bread. He could have been imprisoned for stealing a hen, he knew that, but he had been desperate ... And he was desperate now. Oh dear God, aye he was desperate now – and so was Ben.

Rory realized to what extent Ben was desperate and in fear when he gasped, "My God! not that, not firing."

Of a sudden, Ben pulled him to a halt and gasped again, "Go on. Make to your right. There's ledges and a cave or two near the top. Go in as far as you can and lie low."

"You come an' all."

"Don't be a damn fool, boy. You stay and they'll get us both, and May would rather have half a loaf than no bread."

When Rory didn't move, Ben, on an oath, caught hold of his arm, and once more they were scrambling upwards together.

The second ping hit the rock just above Rory's head, and the shock made him gasp. Then he was gasping, not only from the fact that they were being fired on, but from the sight before his eyes. They were now standing close together, pressed tight against the cliff face, and as the mist cleared for a moment he looked to where, a few feet away, the cliff dropped sheer to the wave-lashed rocks below.

"Listen, boy. Now listen, and do what I say without argument. Go this minute. It's your last chance, for when this mist lifts you'll be a walking target."

"What about you?" Of a sudden Rory felt a deep affection for this man. But whatever he felt, he must stand by him, for strangely he knew that in one way or another Ben had stood by him during the past twenty-four hours.

"Don't worry about me, I know the place like the back of my hand. I can get away on me own, and quick if I'm not hampered. But you, you must take advantage of the mist, so go on straight up the path. Do as I told you before, get hidden and stay there. I'm going straight up over the top." He jerked his head upwards. "There's a path above here only fit for a mountain goat. Go on now." Almost on a laugh he thrust Rory from him. But Rory hadn't taken half-a-dozen reluctant steps along the

114

cliff face path when he swung round on the sound of a stifled groan. Standing transfixed, he saw Ben swaying as he held the side of his neck with both hands while blood gushed through his fingers.

"Oh God! Oh God! Oh God!" He heard himself crying the words aloud; but before he could make any move to help Ben he saw his body sway like the top of a tree in a gentle wind, then slowly fall forward . . .

There was no cry, no sound at all, until he heard a broken splash like a piece of iron makes when it hits the water.

He couldn't move; nor could he see for his eyes were blind with tears; all he could do was moan, "Oh Ben! Ben! Ben!" He had never called him Ben, but once before. Now it was as if he had known him all his life as Ben, Ben his friend.

There was the sound of voices coming up the cliff, excited voices coming nearer, nearer.

He didn't know at what stage he turned and ran; he didn't know he was crying. He didn't realize what he was doing until he too felt himself falling. But the scream that whirled up in him didn't escape his mouth for it was strangled as he landed face forwards into some kind of bush. His face, his neck, his hands and his bare legs between the top of his boots and the bottom of his trousers were so pierced with some spiky form of foliage as to make him want to cry out, but as if Ben were still with him and were guiding him, telling him to make no sound, he lay as he had fallen and kept perfectly still.

There came to him the sound of the sea below him, the sea in which Ben was now lying. The tears spurted afresh from his eyes, and he could make no move to wipe them away, nor did he want to.

Mingled with the sound of the sea now there came men's voices, one quite close, just above him in fact. It was impossible, he thought, that the man could not see him.

115

He heard a voice from a distance shouting, "Can you get down there?" and the voice close to him answering, "Not here. Nowhere along here. We'll have to go back to the cove."

A third voice was shouting now, "Can you see him?"

"No; no sign of him. And I doubt if there will be; the tide will take him out."

"Come down and we'll take the boat out ... You think there was only the one?"

"That's all I saw."

Now the third voice came from well up the cliffs, thin and high, calling, "I'm sure I spotted two of them."

There came to Rory now the sound of scrambling steps, and another voice was joined to the first one that was just above him, and the second voice said, "He'd be on his own; his pal Hawkins left a few weeks ago, got cold feet Crawford said; but he said Bachelor would go on alone for he could handle the boat well. It was only the getting out and in was the trouble."

The other voice answered now, "A pity they didn't all go over the cliffs together. I think she would have preferred it to where they're going. Mind you, I wouldn't give tuppence for Crawford's chances if he's still alive when they get back. Giving the whole show away just because she shot his dog. An' the Captain was right after all to wait. If he had raided the house last week he would have missed this haul."

"Well, he has missed it, hasn't he?" came the other voice. "It's down there, on him."

"Oh, there's a chance yet. We may pick him up as the tide goes out."

There was the sound of scrambling feet above him, and when the sound had faded away he did not move, not even to raise his head. There was in him no inclination to stir even a finger. His body seemed a dead weight. Although he knew he was bleeding in several places it didn't seem to matter. His heart was heavy as lead, more so than ever his body was or could be.

After some time he became aware of full daylight seeping through the tangled bushes above him, and when at last he decided to lift his head and shoulders to find out exactly where he was, he realized that part of his disinclination to move was that he couldn't because of some injury. When he went to put pressure on his left elbow to raise his head the pain was so excruciating that he almost fainted.

What had happened to him? Had he broken his back? His neck? Don't be stupid, he said to himself; try again.

He tried again, with the same result. Something had happened to his arm; he must have broken it. Now what was he going to do? How would he get out of this wherever he was with a broken arm? Well, he must find out. Try his other side. He put pressure on his right elbow and drew in a long breath when he found that he could raise himself a little, but not without sweat-creating pain.

Having pushed his head upwards through the prickly tangle, the sight below him almost made him retch, for he seemed to be dangling in mid-air above sharp-pointed bare rocks. No longer covered with the tide, their nakedness made them appear even more cruel than they had been when Ben's body hurtled towards them.

He drew his head slowly back and took one long slow deep breath; then cautiously, very cautiously, he attempted to push himself back through the tangle towards the face of the cliff, but found this impossible. What he had to do, he knew, was to stand up. He must find out exactly where he was and what chance he had of getting out of it.

Slowly, he swivelled himself round and looked upwards. There above him, about six feet away, was the sloping path from which he had fallen, but as he gazed at it he thought it might as well be sixty feet for he'd never be able to reach it.

He gently eased himself again into the gorse and tried to think. If his arm hadn't been hurt he might have made

118

it because the cliff sloped upwards less steeply here. If it hadn't been so, he realized he would, in his fall, have missed the ledge and the haven of gorse clumps. Well, there was only one thing for it, he'd have to shout for help.

There were two boats some way from the shore. They'd be the Excise men trying to recover Ben's body. Poor Ben! Poor Ben! But he mustn't start bubbling again. What would Ben have done in a position like this, he now asked himself? Would he have yelled to the men down there to come and rescue him? No, no, because he would have thought of the consequences ... transportation.

Sit tight. It was as if Ben was speaking to him. Wait till the boats move off, then get on your feet and see how far you are from the top. In the meantime sit still and save your breath.

He nodded in answer to his own thoughts. Yes, that's what he would do.

The pain in his shoulder was making him sick, and although his clothes were wet he was very dry inside, like he used to be after eating salt herring. It was all the sea water he had swallowed. He would have drowned if it hadn't been for Ben ... He mustn't keep thinking of Ben; he would go to pieces if he thought of Ben.

The sun came out and filtered through the gorse. His head and face felt warm but the rest of his body was shivering. He lay back and closed his eyes, and when next he opened them and peered out to sea through the branches there was no sign of the two boats.

Cautiously, he looked to the right and to the left of him. The cliff curved away on both sides, and he realized that the spot where he was was almost where the cliff jutted out. This, in a way, was an advantage ... Now how to reach that path!

His limbs cramped and trembling, he slowly drew himself upwards. He had no idea how firm was his actual foothold. Standing, he was still breast high in the gorse and when he went to press his way to the actual rock face he found that his thigh, on one side, was impeded by something.

When he put his hand down and felt a small jut of rock his heart gave an excited leap. Once he could get a foot on to that he'd be within reach of the path. But what if he found he couldn't make the haul to the path? ... Well! it was all or nothing, now or never. If he stopped to think anymore he'd get frightened, and if he waited very much longer his limbs would be too stiff to do anything. If only he had the use of his other hand. Well, he hadn't, had he, so he'd better get going, hadn't he?

As if he were being pushed he leant forward against the tangle of branches and pressed one knee through it until it was touching the edge of the foothold. Then, reaching upwards, he grasped a niche in the cliff face and slowly, cautiously, drew up his other leg until the sole of his boot was resting on the tiny ledge. Now, holding his breath, he leant his body against the slope of the cliff, released his one hand hold and groped upwards. The reaction of relief when his fingers came over the edge of the path was almost as disastrous as if he had lost his foothold altogether for, being too confident, he lifted his feet too sharply from the ledge and for a split second found himself dangling in mid-air before his foot found its hold again.

Dear Lord! Dear God! that was a near one.

He lay against the rock gasping for a moment. The position now was, would he have strength enough in his one arm to pull himself up. He doubted it. His eyes moved over the face of the rock. Just in front of him, level with his chin, was a long fissure. If he could bear to press his bad arm on that it might help. But it would all have to be done in one movement; get his elbow into the fissure, press and heave himself onto the path with his good hand.

Taking a deep breath, he raised himself on tip-toe, stretched his body to its full extent, got his left forearm resting on the fissure, put all his strength into the pull of his right arm and heaved his body upwards ... His shoulders were over the top of the rock, his chest was on the path, his belly following, then his legs.

Oh, Thank You God. Thank You God. He had made it. He lay still, his face pressed to the rough uneven surface of the cliff path. Then cautiously he drew himself to his feet and, keeping close to the wall of rock, moved along it. A few yards further on it curved away and sloped gently upwards. Five minutes later his feet touched grass, and there he was, in the field that Ben had spoken of.

He didn't pause to look back down the cliff that had so nearly taken his life, but now, at a shambling run, crossed the field and made for a group of trees at the far side of it.

The trees were the beginning of a stretch of woodland, and he walked on until he came to some thick scrub, and there, lying close under its shelter, he rested and took stock of the situation.

What was he to do? Well, there was one thing he needn't do now, and that was to go back to that house. But what about the ... blue baccy? Until now he had forgotten what he was carrying. Slowly he dropped his gaze to his waistline, then pushed his hand in between his coats. There it was, stuck against his flesh; the little cart-wheel of baccy.

Thank goodness the missis had had the foresight to sew some money into his shirt, he thought now. But he couldn't use it to travel second class, like the way he had come, not in the mess he was in. He would have to go third class, and that was going to be rough. But what matter as long as he got home.

He looked down at himself. His coat was ripped, his trousers scraped almost threadbare at the knees, and the gap between his shoes and trousers showed he had no stockings on. By! he was in a mess. And not only his clothes; there was his arm. He'd have to see a doctor.

The prospect disturbed him. Doctors asked questions.

They would ask where he came from, and he knew he had only to open his mouth to be taken for a foreigner in these parts.

But first things first. He must get two of the half sovereigns out of his shirt.

It took him some time to unpick the stitches from around the little pockets and to unearth the golden coins. Having done so, he got to his feet and started to tidy himself up by straightening his hair and banging his wet coat against a tree but stopped halfway in the process. He must look like a tramp; he could be a tramp. Aye, that was it. There were lots of lads like him on the road going from farm to farm, looking for work. At least they did in the North. But he'd heard tell work was just as hard to get for farm workers down this end of the country. So that's what he'd be, a farm lad looking for work, until he reached a station where it would be safe to get on a train.

He stood up then walked through the woods until he reached a road whose ruts told him that it had once been a coach road, and was still used at times but for narrower vehicles. He walked along it for some miles before he came to a small village.

He could see no name to the village, but it held a blacksmith's shop, an inn and a store, and he noticed from the doorway of the store that it sold almost everything from paraffin oil, stored in a big tin drum, to wicker baskets and rope mats. At the far end of the shop was a counter that held eatables; bread, butter, bacon, cheese. He advanced slowly towards it, and the woman behind the counter watched him and, when he stopped before her, she said, "Well'n what you after, boy?"

"Can ... can I have some cheese, please, and ... and some bread?"

She stared at him. "You're not from these parts?"

"No."

"Where from?"

122

"Oh." He thought for a moment. "London way."

"Ah, thought so; talk like a foreigner. You got money to pay?"

"Yes." He produced the half sovereign, and she looked at it, then at him before saying, "How did you come by that?"

"Workin'."

"Workin'? Where?"

He swallowed and jerked his head. "Back yonder."

"Oh aye, Exmouth way. Pay good money there for off labour, mostly Irish though. You're not Irish?"

"No, no, I'm not Irish."

"Well, what do you want?"

"A piece of cheese please and some bread and butter."

"Half pound cheese? This what's tenpence?"

"Yes, please."

"How much bread? Threepence a loaf – one? two?"

"Oh, I'll only take one loaf."

"Want it sliced?"

"Aye. Yes, please."

After she had sliced the bread and cut the cheese, she said, "Want some tea? Good tea this, sixpence an ounce. Won't get cheaper."

"I . . . I've got nowt to brew it in. Could I have a drink of milk?"

She stared at him for a moment, then said, "You can have a pint for a penny or a quart of skimmed for a ha'penny."

"I'll have a pennorth. Can . . . can I have a piece of bacon an' all?" He nodded towards the ham on the corner of the counter and she replied, "Tenpence a pound that is. A quarter? half?"

"I'll take a pound."

"Pound it is," she said. Coming round the counter, she took up a can and, shooing the flies from the rim of the pail of milk, she dipped the can into it, then handed it to him saying, "No bottle or anything to put it in? You going to drink it now?"

"Aye, I'm thirsty."

She watched him take a long draught of the milk, then said, "What's wrong with your arm?"

"I've hurt it. Sprained it I think."

"You think! Don't you know? Is it broken?" She put out her hand and took hold of his forearm and when he winced visibly she said, "Ted Corbett, he being the blacksmith, he'll tell you what's wrong. Sets bones good as doctor. Wait here a minute and I'll shout him."

Before he could make any protest she went to the shop door and from there she yelled, "You Ted! here a minute!" Then she turned abruptly back into the shop again and said rapidly, "That'll be one an' seven," and as he handed her the half-sovereign she said, "Will I sandwich your cheese and ham for you, twixt the bread?"

"Yes please." He had just finished speaking when the blacksmith strolled into the shop. He wasn't a big man like Mr Morley Cornwallis, but he had breadth. Rory thought he had never seen such a broad man.

"Aye, what is it, Kate?" His voice seemed as broad and as deep as his body, and the woman behind the counter pointed her thumb at Rory and said, "Boy here, summit wrong with his arm. Doesn't know rightly."

"Oh." The man approached Rory. "Well, let's see it boy. Off with your coats." He touched his shoulder. "Ah! Ah!" He nodded. "Painful as that is it? You be in a bit of a mess." He looked at the top coat as Rory dropped it to the shop floor. "Think you'd been in battle. And wet you are. Walking all night?"

Rory blinked and mumbled, took off his other coat, then quickly buttoned the middle button of his shirt, for the blue baccy was rolling loose in the pouch of his shirt now.

When the blacksmith's fingers moved over his shoulder Rory turned his head and looked at them in surprise. They looked horny and hard but their touch was soft, even gentle.

"Ah, nothin' much; slipped out of socket, that's all. One, two, three!"

Rory gave a yelp like a dog in pain; then he stood gasping as he looked from the blacksmith down to his now swinging arm.

"Shoulder out. You fell on it?"

"Aye. Aye I did. But thanks. Thank you very much. What ... what do I owe you?"

"Owe me, boy? Oh!" The blacksmith now stroked his chin thoughtfully, looked at the woman behind the counter, jerked his head at her, then said, "What do you think, Kate? Ten guineas?" Then he gave out a deep bellow of a laugh, in which the woman joined, and Rory was forced to smile.

"If he had a penny for every bone he's set," the woman was saying, "he wouldn't need his anvil any more."

"Thank you, Mister."

"Welcome boy. Where you making for?"

Rory wet his lips, then said, "London."

"Oh, London. Oh boy, you've got a walk before you. Take a week or two to do London."

"Yes, yes, I know." Rory nodded at him, then asked, "Could ... could you put me on the nearest way? They say if you follow a railway line you will make it quicker."

"Aw then, which railway line? You have a choice. They're springing up like mushrooms all over the country. But they tell me 'tis better to drive in a pig truck than in some of them. Were I you, boy, I'd make straight for Honiton; then take road from there that skirts Upottery and ask the way to Taunton. The roads are better there, and there's the railway too. There's plenty on the road that'll put you right." The blacksmith now put his head on one side and said, "You're young to be travelling alone; where's your home?"

"Beyond London."

"You've people then?"

"Aye, they ... they are all out of work."

125

"Well, glad to be of help, boy."

"Thank you, Sir."

The blacksmith turned and smiled at him, then said, "An' thank you, young sir," before walking out, his rumbling laugh shaking his body.

The woman now said, "There, I've put them in a clean sack for you. No charge I'm making for it, no charge. It'll keep the food out of your pockets; not that these pockets would hold what you've got here."

"Thank you, Ma'am. Thank you for your kindness."

"You're welcome, boy, you're welcome. Safe journey. And look you –" she came round the counter again – "put that change where it'll be safe. But if you swallowed it, it still wouldn't be safe from some of the thieves you meet on the road. Be wary, boy, be wary."

"I will, Ma'am, I will. Good-day to you."

"Good-day, boy. You'll find that ham sweet and the bread fresh. Three days it'll keep; it's just out of the oven."

He half turned and nodded to her, then went out and on to the road. But within a moment he was back in the shop again, asking, "Which is the road to Honiton, Ma'am?"

With a spritely step she came out of the shop and standing in the middle of the road she pointed, saying, "Straight on. Follow the river out of Honiton to Upottery. Then just follow your nose and you'll come to Taunton."

"Thank you, Ma'am."

She nodded to him, and he knew that she was watching him as he walked away up the road.

About half-a-mile along the road he went through a gap in a stone wall and, sitting hidden from the road, he made a meal from the contents of the sack. But there was no edge to his appetite; he ate because he knew he'd have to eat if he ever intended to get back to his master. He was only grateful for one thing at the moment, he could now use both his arms. That blacksmith was better than any doctor. He'd remember him for a long time, and with gratitude . . .

. . .

Utterly weary and footsore, he reached Taunton just before dark and enquired the way to the station. Once there, he asked when he could get a train to London Town.

"Not before nine o'clock morrow mornin'," said the porter, curtly.

"Oh!" Rory stared at him blankly before asking, "Is there any place hereabouts where I could sleep?"

The porter looked him up and down; the torn coat, the worn trousers, the two inches of bare flesh above his boots, his dirty face, his tousled hair; then he said, "Shed over there. Holds horse hay. You can get down in that till mornin'. But let's ask you this. Have you the money for a ticket?"

"Aye, yes; but only third class."

"I should think so!" The porter again looked him up and down. "Well, go on, find your way in afore it's dark."

Rory wanted to ask if there was any place he could get a hot drink, but he saw at a glance that the porter wasn't akin to the blacksmith or to the woman in the shop, so he turned away and went towards the outbuilding. And he wasn't ungrateful when he found he could lie on a pile of hay well away from the door.

Before settling down to sleep he once more helped himself to some food from the sack. But it wasn't food he wanted at this moment so much as a drink, a long warm . . . hot, scalding drink, for his body was shivering with the cold.

Once he was snuggled down deep in the hay he thought that he would drop immediately to sleep because he felt so exhausted, but it was some time before sleep came to him. And then it was troubled sleep. He was back on the island; he was sinking into deep, deep water. Someone was firing at him, and the bullet pierced his shoulder blade. The Excise men had got him and were dangling him by a rope over the cliff. He awoke, his hands on his neck, gasping for breath, to find himself almost suffocating in the hay.

He lay looking upwards. Daylight was breaking. He'd have to get up, but he didn't want to move. His body felt heavy and he was no longer cold, in fact he felt hot and his head was aching. The hay was warm and snug, he could quite easily fall asleep again. There was no hurry, he could get another train . . .

What was the matter with him? He sat up in the hay, dusted the pieces from his head and shoulders, slowly got to his feet and banged his hands against his coat and trousers. Then he picked up the sack. He did not open it; he wasn't hungry, all he wanted was a drink.

The porter said, "Hello there! sleep all right?"

"Yes, thank you . . . Do you think it's possible to get a sup of tea or something hot?"

The porter looked at him. Then pointing through the opening into the road, he said, "Along the street there, opposite the hanging sign, you'll get a breakfast for sixpence. You've plenty of time, another hour yet."

"Oh thank you. Thank you."

The eating house was rough and so was the food, a plate of fat bacon and fried bread and a mug of tea. He drank the mug of tea straightaway, ate a little of the fried bread, but couldn't look at the bacon. Then going to the counter he asked if he could have another mug of tea.

"Cost you a penny," said the man.

"All right," he said and handed the extra penny across the counter. Taking the mug back to the wooden bench, he slowly sipped at the tea and wished the time would pass more quickly.

He was back in the station a full twenty minutes before the train was due and was surprised to see the number of respectable-looking people waiting, and those like himself not so respectable-looking. The respectable ones stood in groups on the wooden planks before the booking office, the others stood to the extreme right of the building on the rough cinder track, and it was towards the latter group that he made his way.

When the train was ten minutes late everyone began talking, and fifteen minutes later still when it did arrive, puffing and snorting, he was almost knocked to the back by the rush to the carriages.

When he eventually boarded the train it was in one of the last two compartments, and he saw that it was just a roofless box lined with wooden seats, and all of these were now occupied.

He had considered the journey from London very trying; the wooden seats had tested his bones; but before they had been going many miles he was longing to sit on a wooden seat.

Standing and being jostled here and there like butter in a churn was just one of the discomforts for, depending on the wind, he was choked with smoke and blinded with coal dust. His head began to ache more than ever and his body became hot, and while the other eight passengers in the box were stamping and flapping their hands against the cold, the sweat was running down the inside of his shirt.

When he slid down to the floor in the corner of the box and made no retaliation as a man's boot caught him in the thigh, he thought, I'm bad; I've got a fever. Then fear turned him cold. Had he the cholera?

It wasn't long before he realized that this thought had entered the minds of his companions, for he couldn't believe it when, after the train stopped at yet another station, he had the wooden section to himself, except for one middle-aged woman. She sat near him on the floor and asked, "Are you feeling ill, boy?"

"I'm very hot," he replied.

"Let me look at your tongue."

"What?"

"Put your tongue out."

He put his tongue out. Next, she pulled down his lower lids. Then he tried to shrug away from her when she unbuttoned his two coats and even his shirt and put her hand on his bare flesh. But, looking into her face, which was kindly and firm he did not thrust her off. When she had buttoned up his shirt and his coats she patted his arm, saying, ""Tisn't cholera."

"How d'you know?"

"I've seen a lot of cholera. You've got a chill, a feverish chill. You ought to be in bed. Have you got far to go?"

He stared into her face for a moment. "The North," he said, "Durham way."

"Oh! Durham way. Which part?"

"Outside of Hebburn and Jarrow."

"Oh, near South Shields."

"Aye." His eyes widened a little. "Do you know that part?"

"Very well, boy, very well. I worked in the mission there for years."

That's why she was kind. She was one of these missionary ladies. He felt relaxed somehow, safe.

She said now, "Go to sleep if you can; we have another four hours before us."

And, strangely, he went to sleep and when he woke up it was to find that he had his head on her shoulder.

At one time she said to him, "How much money have you got?" which caused him to stiffen slightly until she went on, "If you have enough to travel second class it would be better for you," and he said, "I've enough if they'll let me go, looking like this."

"If you've got the money for the ticket I'll see you go second class."

"Thank you, Ma'am."

Afterwards, when he looked back, he couldn't remember at what time they reached London; he only

130

knew that he was riding on a horse bus for the first time and he was too tired to enjoy it. Then he was entering a grim stone building and the woman in the black dress, she was not wearing her cloak and bonnet now, was actually putting him to bed. But when she tried to slip off his trousers and shirt he fought her. When her hand touched his waist and she gathered up the hidden circle and said, "What's this?" he slapped at her, saying, "Leave me be. Leave me be, 'tis only baccy. I'm taking it home for me da."

"All right, boy, all right," she answered quietly, "nobody's going to touch it, or you. Go to sleep."

And he went to sleep, but lying flat on his stomach and willing his fuddled mind not to allow him to turn over . . .

He was still lying on his face when she was there again, still in the black dress. "Come on, sit up and drink this," she was saying. "Are you feeling better?"

Slowly he turned over. His body was aching but his head was clearer. "Yes," he said. "Yes, Ma'am, I'm feeling better."

"Drink this tea."

He drank the tea while she sat on the edge of the bed and watched him; then she said, "Get into your clothes, I've brushed them and sewn your coat; you'll look a little more presentable now. There's a washhouse downstairs. Go down and wash your face and hands and have something to eat. And I don't think you'd better dawdle. The train leaves Euston at half-past seven."

"Oh." His face moved into a stiff smile. "Thank you, Ma'am. Thank you ever so kindly."

"You must give me your address before we part boy; some day I'll be coming your way and I'll expect hospitality from you."

"Yes, Ma'am, yes, Ma'am. And you'll get it."

"I'm sure I shall, boy." She now got up and with short brisk steps walked out of the small cell-like room.

Less than an hour later he was sitting on the hard seat

131

near the window of the second class compartment. His other side was pressed tightly against a stout lady, which position he found strangely comforting. Outside on the rude platform, stood the lady in the black cape and bonnet. Mrs Wheatley, she said her name was. He felt as he looked at her that he was parting with a life-long friend, yet twenty-four hours ago he hadn't known she was alive.

Before he left the Mission House he had taken the last two half sovereigns from his shirt and had asked her to change one, and when she had done this he had offered her two shillings, and she had accepted them gratefully and dropped them into a box chained to the wall inside the front door of the house.

A whistle blew, there was a noise of escaping steam, the couplings clanged and the train moved away. He waved to her and she waved to him. "We'll meet again," she called, and he nodded at her.

Funny, but he wouldn't mind meeting her again. He'd heard funny things about missionary ladies, always ranting on about God and hell fire, but she had never once mentioned either of them. No, he wouldn't mind meeting her again. He leaned back against the hard wooden back of the compartment. He was going home. He was going home. He was going home. The wheels were beating it out faster and faster. He was going home.

Chapter Seven

He slipped from the back of the carrier's cart at the crossroads and Frank Jackson called to him, "Will you be able to find your way, lad?" and he replied curtly, "Blindfold."

He didn't like Frank Jackson; he had never liked Frank Jackson. He stood in the middle of the road watching the tail light of the cart swinging away into the distance. He was home, he was home. It was like a song on a hurdy-gurdy churning inside him. All the way from London he could think of nothing else but that he was going home, and now he was home.

He lifted his head and sniffed the air. It was different; sharper, thinner, colder, fresher – different ... And he was different.

Slowly he turned about and walked along the narrow ridged road that would take him to the open fell. He had only been away for a week, seven days in all, but he was different; he'd never be the same again.

He knew now that when he had left here he'd been a lad, a boy, but now, no matter what he might look outside, inside he was like a man, because it wasn't age that made a man, but experience, the experience of people. And he couldn't count the different types of people he had met during the last seven days, both good and bad.

He gauged the spot to leave the road and to climb the bank on to the higher land. Ten minutes later he knew he was nearing the burn and that it was running strongly, for its gurgling was louder than usual. There must have been some heavy rain during the past week, he guessed. He sought and found the stepping stones and was congratulating his judgment in hopping from one to the other when his foot slipped and he went into the water. Usually, it would have just reached his knees, but he found that it was swirling round his waist, besides which it was icy cold. But what did it matter? He was actually laughing as he pulled himself up the bank. Nevertheless, he shivered violently as he walked on again. He would have liked to run to keep himself warm, but that was too risky. He might trip over some small outcrop of rock and stun himself. It had been known. Just two years gone they had found a man frozen to death out here by just doing that, tripping over a rock and stunning himself.

Of a sudden he stopped. He could see the village, pin points of dim light in the blackness. He was near the road.

When he reached the road he did run. He ran until he neared the first cottages. Then he brought his running to a steady walk, a walk that befitted someone returning from a journey, a dangerous journey. By aye! he could say that again, and in truth.

He cast a glance towards the blacksmith's shop. The door was open and inside there was a dim glow from the banked down fire, and a brighter glow from the window in the cottage next door. There was a warm light coming from the Grey Hen public house and a dim light from the back room of Mrs Beeney's shop. He saw that Miss Tyler was still hard at work with her dressmaking for her lamp was bright, and she only turned it full up when she was working. And there at the end of the street was the house he looked upon as home, the wheelwright's shop. There were lights coming from both the upper front window and the side one.

His heart began to beat faster with excitement as he neared the yard, but when he entered it he paused a moment at the sight of a cart standing there. A cart in the yard shouldn't have been an unusual sight except that this one was ready for the road with a horse in the shafts, and standing to the side of the horse, holding the reins, was Sammy.

He had almost reached the boy before Sammy recognized him, and then with a spring the child was in his arms, clinging to his neck and crying, "Oh our Rory! Oh our Rory! Our Rory!"

"Here!" Rory laughed gently as he patted the back of his head. "What's up?"

The child, pressing himself slightly away from him and looking into his face, gulped through his tears. "I thought you was dead. Everybody thought you was dead."

"Me dead? What made you think that?"

"Well, the man —" he jerked his head towards the trap — "he came yesterda' and he's in there again pesterin' the missis. I don't like him and she doesn't like him; she blames him for Mr Cornwallis dyin'."

Slowly Rory let the boy slide from his arms, then stood looking down at him before he whispered, "What did you say?"

Sammy made no reply, and Rory said again, "The master, he's dead?"

"Aye, Rory; he ... he went yesterda' afternoon, sudden like, after the man had been."

"Oh no! no!" Rory shook his head and as he did so his hand went to his waist and gripped the circular lump underneath his coats. Blue baccy. He had brought it back and the master was dead. Two men that he had liked were dead, one he could say he more than liked, for in a secret way he had loved Mr Cornwallis more than his

135

father. Both bad men, some people would say, because they were mixed up with the law, but ... nobody was all black and nobody was all white. "What do you say?" he looked down at Sammy.

"I heard the man say that if you did come back the missis had to send word over to some place right away. I couldn't get the name, but it's in Gateshead."

Before Sammy had finished speaking there came the sound of voices from the back room of the shop and Rory, bending down, whispered hastily, "Listen Sammy, say nowt. Do you understand? Say nowt at all till that man's gone. Don't tell the missis I'm back, either, just keep mum."

"Aye, Rory; but ... but where you goin'?"

"Just into the shed over there. I'll hide till he's left."

"Aye, Rory."

Rory now dashed across the yard and into the shed, and within two minutes he saw, coming out of the back door of the shop, a man in a high bowler hat and a heavy overcoat. He watched him get up into the trap, then turn and look towards the door and say, "Now don't forget, let me know. It'll be very worth your while." Then he looked down at Sammy and shouted, "Out of the way, boy!" before urging the horse forward.

Rory waited some minutes before moving. As he left the shed Mrs Cornwallis's voice came from the doorway, saying, "Come in, child." But when Sammy didn't move she came into the yard, saying, "Do you hear me, boy?"

"Missis."

Rory watched his mistress's hands go to the front of her blouse and grip it, and when he stood in front of her her whole face trembled so much she was unable to speak for a moment. Then she said softly, "It's you boy?"

"Aye, Missis."

"You're safe." Her hands were on his head, moving down his face and over his shoulders, and of a sudden he found that he was in her arms, being held tightly to her; and in turn he put his arms about her and held her.

Then she had him by the hand, saying hastily, "Come in. Come away in."

They didn't speak again until they were in the sitting room. There, in the light of the lamp, she looked him up and down, and her hand went to her cheek as she said, "Oh boy! boy! what a state you're in. Your new clothes almost in rags. And ... and you're wet." She looked down at her own apron now, that had soaked up some of the water from his clothes, and she said hastily, "Get them off, boy. Get them off." And as she went to take off his coat she suddenly stopped and, looking into his face, said, "Are ... are you all right, I mean in yourself? You don't look well."

"I'm all right. But Missis –" he stopped before taking off his jacket – "Sammy tells me –" He moved his eyes towards the bedroom door, and Mrs Cornwallis lowering her head and, the tears flowing down her face now, said, "Yes, boy, he went yesterday. Yet it's God's will, God knows best. Perhaps it's as well he went like that for the doctor tells me he would never have moved out of that bed again, and that alone would have killed him shortly. There's only one thing I'm sorry for, he ... he went thinking that he had done you an injury, in fact sent you to your death. But we'll talk no more, boy, until you get those wet things off. Sammy!" She turned to the small boy. "Go to the blanket box and bring me two out."

"Aye, Missis."

When the boy had gone from the room Mrs Cornwallis, suddenly taking Rory's hands in hers, gripped them as she said, "Oh boy! Oh boy, I'm so glad to see you."

"And me you, Missis."

They stared at each other in silence for a moment before she said, "You'll be hungry. I'll get you something hot, and ... and then we must talk. There's a lot to be said, isn't there?"

Rory made no answer to this, he just moved his head once.

Chapter Eight

It was well after midnight when Rory, moving gently away from Sammy's side, slid to the floor and groped for the candlestick. When he had lit the candle he pulled a blanket round him; then, stretching out his hand, he took from under the straw mattress the round flat circle of tobacco. Crouching on the floor, he sat gazing at it and the question sprang at him, as it had done a number of times since he had come back to the house, why had he not told the missis about it?

Last night, after he had eaten and Sammy had been sent upstairs, the missis had taken him into the bedroom where his master was laid out, not looking dead at all but just peacefully asleep, and once again he had let the tears run down his face.

Later, in the sitting room, he had sat side by side with the missis before the fire and, breaking a long silence, she had said, "He was a good man, boy. No matter what you have learned, he was a good man." And to this he had replied, "Yes, Missis, I know."

"He trapped himself for life in one drinking bout, but from that day strong liquor never passed his lips. He was a good man." Then abruptly and in a changed tone she had asked, "Did you meet her?" and he nodded.

"Aye, Missis. And I didn't like her. She's ... she's a bad woman."

"I'm with you there," she had said; then went on, "It wasn't until you were gone that Mr Cornwallis realized that she might try to trap you as she had done so many others."

"She did, Missis," he said.

"Well, I doubt if she'll trap any more. Did you know they were caught?"

"Aye," he said. "I gathered as much when I was on that ledge and I heard them talking – somebody called Peter Crawford gave them away."

"Yes," she said, "Peter Crawford. He was an old man and had worked for her for years. Mr Cornwallis often spoke of him."

To his question, "How did you come to know she was caught?" she had replied, "Him, the man you saw leaving last night, he came yesterday morning bringing the papers; it was all in there. All about the militia and the Excise men waiting for the boat coming in."

"What'll happen to her?" he had asked.

"Only God and the law know that. But she'll get her deserts. An' I'm tellin' you, there'll be many a mind set at ease this night knowing that they're free from her clutches. The London paper that man had was full of it, but one item alone brought him here. When they picked up the body of Ben Bachelor they found half a necklace on him made of very precious stones. It was wedged inside the baccy and it were worth a lot of money. He came to find out if Mr Cornwallis had got back with the other half. When he found him in bed he raged on until John told him that you had been sent in his place. Then this evening when he came to see if there was any news of you, he showed no sorrow that my man had died. There were some good men involved in this business, but there were also some bad ones, and he is one of them, I'd say." And she had ended, "Well, boy, he'll be back, and all you've got to say to him is you know

140

nothing about it. You were taken to the island and you were brought back and you managed to get away. And thank God for that much anyway. You just speak the truth."

Speak the truth. Why hadn't he there and then said, "I've got the other half of that necklace, it's upstairs under the mattress?" Why hadn't he? Because as he had looked at her he knew that by telling her he'd be heaping more worry on her.

With the death of her husband, she imagined the worry and anxiety of being concerned in the blue baccy intrigue was finished, but he knew he had only to produce that little brown cart-wheel and it would all start up again. And her worry would be for him now, for, once he handed it to that man, he would be as much in the thick of it as if May Bluett had trapped him for life. He had been carrying stolen goods. He had gone over to Jersey by night and had returned by night. The man would take the place of May Bluett and would force him into the blue baccy game.

Slowly now he pulled the end of the roll of baccy away from a cleft in the twist, and gently began to straighten it out. But no sooner had he exposed the inner coil than he stopped and, with finger and thumb gently poised, plucked from the bed of the tobacco a bright stone. After gazing at it for a moment he laid it down gently on the bare wooden floor, then picked up another, and another. As he unwound towards the middle of the coil the stones, he saw, became gradually larger, and when he reached the heart of it, there, taking up more than half the width of the baccy, and blinking as if just waking from sleep, was a different stone.

This stone gave off a soft reddy-pink glow and was twice the size of the biggest of them. Prising it from its nest, he placed it in the hollow of his hand and gazed at it. It was bonny, beautiful. Lily would love something like this. His fist closed on it just in time to stop it rolling on the floor. *Enough of that.* By lad! Aye, enough of that.

But what was he going to do with this lot? His throat was dry. The very sight of them lying there in a little heap began to fill him with fear ... Anyway, one thing he was certain of; that bloke wasn't getting them. Another thing was, he couldn't tell, or he wasn't ever going to tell, the missis about them. He would hide them, and later on, perhaps years ahead, he could take the stones one by one over a period of time into Newcastle and sell them. They would make sure that he and his folks would never know want again – aye and they might make sure he'd find himself in trouble. A jewellery man would have a way of asking questions as to how an ordinary fellow such as himself came by diamonds. Because this is what they were, diamonds. All except the middle one. He didn't know what this one was.

Well what was he going to do with them?

Bury them.

No, if he buried them he would be tempted some time to go and dig them up. He stared into the darkness beyond the rim of light afforded by the candle, and the answer came to him, and he replied to it firmly in his head, "Aye, aye, that's what I'll do." He gathered up the stones but he did not return them to their nest in the tobacco, instead he bundled them into a piece of coarse linen, which he pushed under the mattress. Then he straighened out the roll of baccy and pushed that under the mattress. Cut into bits, old Peter Tollett and Benny Croft would be glad of that; he could tell them he bought it in London ... 'twould be a lie but a lie that hurt nobody.

He got into bed, and his last thought before he went to sleep was, I wonder what the morrow'll hold?

. . .

The first thing the morrow held was Mr Morley Cornwallis and Bernie. He was sitting at the table having

142

his breakfast when they came in unannounced, startling even Mrs Cornwallis. She turned from the fire, saying, "Why Morley! Why, you're early."

"Not early enough to get some folks out of bed!" Morley Cornwallis threw a hard glance at Rory. Then looking again at Mrs Cornwallis, he said, "I'll be goin' into Shields, Rosie, and wonder if you've changed your mind about them funeral arrangements."

"No, I have not, Morley," replied Mrs Cornwallis harshly. "And I'm not likely to at this stage. It was all settled yesterday. Robson's are laying him to his rest, plumed hearse, three coaches an' all."

Rory saw the muscles on Morley Cornwallis's face tighten. He watched him shake his head slowly as he said, "'Twouldn't have been John's wish to throw good money away. Bailey's would have done it for half the price, nine pounds coffin an' all."

"Well he wanted no coffin, as you know yourself; he's had his coffin made these fifteen years, and of the best oak. The tree picked by himself, no valley bottom stuff. And he's seen it polished every year since, as he has mine. And he's not havin' any cheap cabs to match good oak, he's goin' to be put away proper."

"Well, well." Morley Cornwallis's voice had a conciliatory note now. "It's your business, Rosie. After all, it's your business. I'm only thinkin' of your future and money that you're likely to be in sore need of, for you won't be able to keep the shop. You know that much."

Mrs Cornwallis now ground the black kettle into the heart of the fire before she turned about and said, "Whatever much I know, an' whatever you'd like to know, Morley, we'll have to wait till Monday come and his wishes will be read out after he's laid to his rest."

"You back then from your holiday?"

Rory turned his head swiftly and looked up at Bernie Cornwallis who was wearing the usual sneer on his face, and he said, "Aye, I'm back. At least I think I am."

143

"None of your lip."

"Who's lippin'."

They had both forgotten where they were for the moment, until Mrs Cornwallis said, "Enough! enough! an' the master still in the next room."

Wagging his head, Morley Cornwallis looked at Rory now and said, "Time you were at work, boy, isn't it? Whole village is at it as I came along."

"Morley!" Mrs Cornwallis's voice was quiet, but it had a compelling note as it uttered the name, and Morley Cornwallis bowed his head and raised his hand and said, "All right, all right, you know best," on which he turned about and went from the room. But Bernie stood for a moment longer surveying Rory through narrowed eyes, and then he said, "Think you've got it all your own way now, don't you? Surprise comin' to you."

"That wouldn't surprise me," replied Rory, flippantly now; then looked apologetically at Mrs Cornwallis, and she, moving towards the door, said quietly, "Your da's gone, Bernie. Be on your way."

When the door had closed, Mrs Cornwallis looked at Rory's bowed head and said, "Some folks are right inquisitive; they'd have you in a shroud afore you were dead. Look at me, boy."

Rory looked at her, and she went on, "I've no need to ask you to keep your own counsel about the late happenings, have I, boy?" And to this he answered, "No, Missis; you know you haven't, no need at all."

. . .

By eleven o'clock that morning he had answered the questions of Peter Tollett and Benny Croft by giving them a detailed account of his travels and creating a fictitious mother for his late master – which story had Mrs Cornwallis's blessing. He had answered the inquisitive queries of Jim Hoggart as he stood nonchalantly outside the open door of the bar. He had satisfied Mrs Beeney and Miss Tyler, and many others with his explanation. And he had also waved to Lily as she was passing down the street on some message or other. When she hadn't stopped he had known that either her father or Bernie was somewhere in the vicinity with his eyes on her.

But all this he knew was marking time; and at twelve o'clock when Sammy came pelting into the yard and up to him, hissing, "That trap's comin' up the road, Rory, the same one," he knew that the ordeal he was dreading was close upon him.

"All right, all right." Rory bent down now and whispered quietly, "Listen, our Sammy, an' stop lookin' so scared. You know what I told you. When the man asks where I am say I'm down in the field feedin' Scape, all right?"

"Aye, Rory."

"Good." Rory now let himself out the back way and on to the common land where, in the distance, the goat was tethered. He picked up a turnip from a pile lying near the wall and went over the grass, calling, "Here! Scape. Here! Scape."

The goat came trotting towards him as far as its tether allowed, and when Rory reached it, he went down onto his hunkers and held out the turnip. As the goat munched he talked to it, saying, "Been a good lass? Aye, but of course you have; nobody to let you away to go and get drunk, was there? By! by! who would believe it, a nice lass like you gettin' mortallious. Aw, don't start slobbering over me." He pushed the whiskered face gently to one side. Then parting the hair, he looked at the bare patches here and there, old scars healed over, and he shook his head. Mr Cornwallis had done that. He couldn't really believe it ... But then the master hadn't thought it up in the first place; some bright devil must have used goats for years as a means of passin' such cargo. It was clever, he had to give them that. And it never escaped in the daytime, only at night, as Ben had

145

said. In the daytime someone might have collared it. But it was sent back in the daytime, staggering in its walk and the butt and laughter of everybody who saw it. Poor old Scape.

"Hi, boy!"

He took no notice.

"I say, hi boy! Do you hear?"

He had his back to the man. He put his head down and nuzzled Scape playfully and it wasn't until the man called for the third time "You boy!" that he turned on his hunkers towards him, saying, "Aye, Mister, you want me?" Having decided to play the dolt, he sounded definitely like one to himself.

"You Rory McAlister?"

"Aye, Mister." He still kept fondling the goat's head while holding the turnip in his other hand.

"Get up and listen to me. I want to talk to you."

"Aye, Mister."

"John ... your master, Mr Cornwallis, sent you on a journey, didn't he?"

"Oh aye, Mister; right down to the West Country in the train. Oh, awful that was. Part way crushed I was, an' seats no wider than that." He measured about a foot with his hand. "An' stopped at every station comin' back, it did, all day ..."

"Be quiet, boy!" The man peered at him now through narrowed lids, then said, "I'm not interested in the discomforts of your journey. Now listen carefully and answer these questions truthfully. You went to an island in a boat with a man called Ben Bachelor, didn't you?"

"Aye, Mister. He was all right, Ben, nice man."

"You met a number of people on the island?"

"Aye, Mister, and nice family an' all ..."

The man cut him short again and made an impatient movement with his head. "When you were leaving the island what did the family ... I mean the man of the house give to Ben ... Ben Bachelor, can you remember?"

"Oh aye, Mister." He grinned widely now at the man,

146

then ticked off on his fingers, "Two big rolls of baccy, three bottles o'whisky, two bottles o'rum an' a box o'snuff. He wanted me to try the snuff." He laughed now, letting his mouth drop wide. The man waited, and when he didn't go on he asked, "Yes, and what else?"

"That's all, Mister. And dangerous it was, 'cos it was smugglin'."

"Did ... did you see the other man give Ben some small packages, just big enough to put in his coat."

Rory looked to the side, then down at the goat's head, then back at the man, and he screwed up his face as if deep in thought before saying, "No, no, Mister. Tell the truth, Mister, can't remember much 'cos we'd all had cider. By! it was lovely cider. Had a party we had, singin'."

"Be quiet!"

He bridled, then forced himself to keep to the role he had taken on and said docilely, "Aye, Mister."

He watched the man rub his chin and mutter something; then with a quick movement he came close to him and gripped the front of his jacket, saying tensely, "Did you see a small circle of tobacco, about that big?" He measured the exact width of the cart-wheel with his fingers. "Flat baccy, rolled up?"

"No, Mister, no little rolls, only a big one. 'Twould have been daft to bring little uns back after that journey. But I was well away I was, had a drop, all had a ..."

Now gripping his shoulders, the man shook him until his head bobbed and he had the urge to spring back and land him one. Even when he was pushed away he forced himself to stand for some minutes, his hands limp by his sides. Then he asked, "Was it best baccy, Mister, the little one?"

The man now closed his eyes for a moment, then spoke as if to himself, saying, "Two little ones, and they only found one. At least that's what they say. The cunning swine!"

"Who, Mister? Who's cunnin' swine?"

"Oh, be quiet!" The man made an impatient movement with his forearm. Then becoming still and gazing at Rory, he said, "John must have been mad to send you. But then, on the other hand, no. No, I can see his point; it was clever in a way."

"What was clever, Mister?"

"Aw, shut up!" As the man spoke he swung round and aimed his foot towards the goat, and it was only Rory's quick action in grabbing the tether and pulling it aside that saved the animal from the blow, and forgetting his pose for a moment he yelled at the man, "Do that again if you dare and see what you . . ."

Startled by his tone the man's lids again narrowed, and Rory, pulling himself up just in time, knelt on the ground and, putting his arms around the animal, looked up into the thin hard face and drawled now in the tone of his assumed character, "Well, she's mine see. I mean I look after her, I do . . ."

The man stood for a moment longer, then with a quick shake of his head he turned about and marched across the field and so through the doorway into the yard.

Rory remained where he was until, about five minutes later, he heard the trap leave the yard and the horse go at a quick trot up the village street. Then he drew in a deep breath and as he went towards the house he thought, that part's done. I doubt if I'll see him again.

Now he had only to dispose of the blue baccy and the events of this strange week would be closed for ever. He would do it on his way home this afternoon; aye, he would and get it over.

. . .

But he didn't dispose of the blue baccy on his way home that afternoon. His idea had been to drop the stones into the running burn, but when he arrived at the burn the water had gone down and the bottom was clear for as far as he could see on both sides of the stepping stones. Were he to drop them in they would merely lie in the silt, or on the rock bottom, and he would always know they were there and be tempted to retrieve them. So he left them where they were inside his shirt and hurried on his way home to deliver his good news to his family, for his master's word was to be kept. "When you come back," he had said, "your people will have a decent house."

Long before he opened the door he heard his father coughing, and it seemed that nothing had changed in the room since he had entered it nine days ago, except that their faces showed that they were more glad than usual to see him, if that were possible.

The greetings over, he emptied the food from the sacks on to the table, Edna and Mabel standing by his side, their eyes rivetted as usual on the wonderful sight.

"We were beginning to worry about you, boy," said his mother, "and wondered how Sammy was getting along. Is everything all right?"

Rory went now and sat on the foot of his father's bed and, looking from one to the other, he said, "Sammy's all right, Ma, doing fine. Found his feet in fact. But ... but the master, he's gone."

"Gone!" Both his father and mother repeated the word, and he nodded at them. "Aye, he died on Thursday. When ... when I got back, after I had been here afore, when was that? a week Thursday, he'd had an accident. The tree in the saw pit had slipped and fallen on him and broken his back. He died last Thursday."

"Aw no! Aw no!" His mother was shaking his head. And now he saw the fear in her eyes, that wiped out any sorrow for the master's passing. But he understood it, and he said quickly, "But I'm all right, Ma, I'm going to be kept on. The missis says I am. I know nothin' more than that, only she's given me her word that I'm goin' to be kept on. And Sammy an' all. Morley Cornwallis, you know I've told you about him, he thinks the shop will have to be sold now the master's gone, but Mrs

Cornwallis won't have it. I don't know what's goin' to happen really until after the funeral, only that's what she said. 'Don't worry, boy,' she said, 'your job's safe.' And another thing, Ma. The master promised —" he stopped. There was no need to tell them why the master had promised him this reward. To them he had just been doing his ordinary job during the past week, so he said, "We . . . we got talkin', the master and me, and . . . and I told him . . . well, about this." He rolled his eyes round indicating the room, then went on, "and he said you could have a cottage, it's come vacant. It's just outside the village. It's got three rooms, and only the kitchen has a stone floor. There's a patch of land too, and it's bonny, real bonny." His voice ended on a high note.

They looked at him, stared at him in silence, the four of them; only the baby in the basket made any sound, a weak whimpering; and then his mother came and lowered herself slowly down onto the bed by his side and, gripping his hand, she said, "Is this true, boy?"

"Aye, yes, of course it's true. I wouldn't say else would I?" He turned his face from her and looked towards his father, and his father, after staring at him for a moment longer, put his hands suddenly across his eyes, and so Rory, getting to his feet in pretended temper, said, "Well now! nice welcome for good news, isn't it? What do you say, our Edna? Going to have a garden and a nice house, and you can come and feed the goat . . . aw goodness me! Well, did you ever!"

Edna who had run to her mother and buried her head in her lap, was crying too. She was only five years old but she was already aware that paradise was a three-roomed cottage away from the town with two rooms that had wooden floors.

"Come here, son."

He went to his father, and Peter McAlister took both his hands in his own and with difficulty began to speak. "I don't know, lad, how . . . how you brought this about, but masters, no matter how good, well, I know they don't give cottages to apprentices for nothin'. What did you do, boy, to get us out of this hovel?"

Rory blinked and he stared down at his father. His father was difficult to lie to; he had an astute mind, so he said simply, "I went a message for him."

"A message, boy?"

"Aye. It was a long way off, right down in the West Country."

"Down in the West Country?" Peter McAlister moved his head twice. "And did you carry the message successfully?"

As Rory stared at his father, unable to answer, the stones seemed to pierce the linen of the bag and prick his skin, and he said, "You could say I did, Da. Mrs Cornwallis is satisfied anyway."

"What was the message?" His mother was speaking now, and he turned to her for a moment, then looked back at his father before answering, "It's a long story, Da. I'll tell you some of it sometime." He smiled now and bent forward. "Come Christmas like, eh, when you're all settled in, an' the fire's roarin'. Come Christmas I'll tell you."

Peter McAlister now put his hand up and touched Rory's face and said softly, "You're a good lad, Rory. Come Christmas then, come Christmas."

He turned quickly away from his father. Perhaps by Christmas his father wouldn't be there. And he didn't feel a good lad; he wouldn't feel good with himself until he was rid of the blue baccy. He still thought of the stones as being blue baccy.

He said now, "The master'll be buried on Monday. Mistress says I can come and help you move Tuesday. It will mean our Bill gettin' up a bit earlier in the morning', say around five o'clock. But he can ride some of the way in; there's a carrier picks up some workers around six at the crossroads."

"Oh –" his mother smiled widely at him – "Bill won't mind that; he'll be over the moon."

Somewhere in the back of Rory's mind there stirred the thought that it was odd that his nine year old brother would be over the moon because he had to get up at five o'clock in the morning and put three more miles on his journey to work, six miles more a day. He'd have to do something about Bill. His hand went to his waist. The answer to Bill's problem, to all their problems, lay just here, right here.

"What is it, lad?" asked his mother. "You look miles away."

"Oh, nothing, Ma, nothing." He shook his head. "I was just thinking."

. . .

Not a waking hour passed during the next two days but Rory thought of the stones he carried inside his shirt. He daren't leave them under the mattress during the day in case the missis, trying to ease her grief by a bout of house cleaning, should find them. Even in ordinary times she would often turn the bedding when there was apparently no need for it.

So the stones lay against his flesh, a constant reminder that he had to get rid of them. Yet, at the same time, a constant temptation. He admitted the latter to himself quite frankly, for the temptation was strong in him to bury them as an insurance against future want. There would be no need, he had told himself, to try to sell them in Newcastle, he could go up to London. He knew his way about now. And although he would never hope to get half of what one of the stones was worth, he was sure he'd get a price that would represent a small fortune to him.

He could, he told himself, make up some story as to how he came by the stones. There were all kinds of stories he could tell, and over the years he'd be able to pick from them a cast-iron one.

There was no reason at all why he shouldn't bury the

stones, and there was more than one reason why he should. One big and growing reason was that, when he married Lily, and he knew that some day he would marry her, he'd be able to give her nice things and a nice home . . .

The stones, he thought, were getting between him and his wits, for as he walked behind the third plumed carriage alongside Benny Croft, his head bowed, his heart heavy with sorrow, he still couldn't get his mind off the fact of what lay against his flesh.

As he knelt in the church and looked across the aisle at the missis, who was deeply in sorrow, he asked himself, "What's up with you, Rory McAlister? Have you lost every scrap of decency that was in you afore you went on that journey?"

And it seemed proved to him that he had, for when the coffin, borne by six stout men, was carried to the grave, there he was, his mind still taken up completely with the thought of the blue baccy. They were like a curse those stones. They got into you, changing you, making you see bad as good, for his mind was telling him now that it wasn't a bad thing to do to provide for his people in the future.

He stood on one side of the grave and looked across to where the missis, her head bowed, her hand across her mouth, was crying silently, while by her side Mary Ann Morley Cornwallis cried loudly for all to hear. Crocodile tears and make-game moans, thought Rory. What did she really care about the master being gone?

And what do you care, boy, about me being gone?

It was as if the master's voice were coming up out of the grave itself, forcing its way through the clods of earth that were dropping on to the coffin lid.

They were leading the missis away from the grave now and the people were following, but he still stood looking down into the hole. It was weird, frightening; it was as if the master had spoken to him and was still speaking to him from out of his coffin. "You know right from wrong, boy. You've seen the evidence of it in the past few days. Think carefully. The blue baccy will bring you money and with money you can buy almost anything, but one thing you can't buy, the thing that a man needs most – peace of mind.''

He saw the three coaches moving off towards the gates and he made no move to follow them, but cutting between the gravestones, he left the churchyard by a side gate and within a short time he was up on the fell lands, walking fast one minute, running the next.

He knew now what he had to do, and he knew he had to do it at once.

Half-a-mile east of the village the burn ran into the Don, and the Don filled up from the river Tyne, and at high tide it ran fast. But even if the stones weren't washed down to the sea and just sank straight to the bottom, they'd be buried in deep, black, slimy mud and you might dig until you were pink-eyed and never find one, if it were as large as a brick never mind the size of a pea.

When he reached the top of the hill he looked towards the village and saw the black cabs lined up outside the wheelwright's shop. They were back then, and everybody would be inside eating and having a drink of spirits, which was usual at such times.

He crossed the top of the hill and dropped down the other side to the main road, but he had scarcely gone a dozen steps along it when he heard his name called. ''Rory! Rory!''

When he looked back, he saw Lily. She was running fast and holding up her skirts.

Panting, she came up to him but couldn't speak for a moment; then she gasped, ''I . . . I looked for you. You weren't behind. And . . . and then I saw you goin' up the hill. Where . . . where you goin'?''

''To the River.''

''The River? What for?''

Could he tell her? No, no, he doubted if she would

154

believe him. She would think he had gone barmy.

"You all right, Rory?"

"Aye, I'm all right."

"Well, what d'you want to go to the Don for, and now when you should be back in the house givin' a hand?"

"I . . . I've got to do something."

"At the Don?"

"Aye, at the Don."

She stared into his face, then said quietly, "Then I'll come along of you."

He looked at her for a long moment before turning away and walking on, and he made no protest when she walked by his side. They were nearing the burn when she spoke, and then she asked softly, "You in trouble, Rory?"

"Not now," he said, "leastways I won't be in a short while." He was looking ahead when he asked, "Did you get your new frock?"

"Aye, Rory."

"Have you seen Frank Jackson, I mean on his own?"

"He . . . he called in yesterday."

"An' . . . an' you wore your new frock?"

"Aye. Aye, Rory; me ma made me."

"But you'll still keep your promise?"

"Yes, Rory, I'll still keep me promise. When he asks me I'll say no."

They walked on now, past a farm, then another until, going over a hill, they saw the church of St Paul's and the few white-washed cottages that bordered the river. Between the cottages and them stood the little stone bridge on the lonely stretch of road that connected East Jarrow to Jarrow proper.

Standing in the middle of the bridge, close to the parapet, Rory looked about him. He could see no one but an old man approaching in the distance. He looked over the bridge and down into the water. The tide was running high. He put his hand inside his coat, opened the buttons of his shirt, then drew out the linen bag.

Having laid it on top of the narrow parapet, he stared at it for a full minute before he looked at Lily and said, "Will you promise on God's oath that you'll not tell anybody about what I'm goin' to do ... not anybody, not a livin' soul?"

Lily stared lovingly back into his eyes. "I'll promise anythin' you want me to, Rory."

Somehow this wasn't enough for him. She was promising out of affection; he wanted something stronger but he couldn't put a name to it. He wanted to say to her, "Swear an oath!" but what he said was, "If you tell anybody, anybody at all, you'll get me into trouble, awful trouble."

"I'd never get you into trouble, Rory, you know that. Nohow I wouldn't. I've no need to swear to it."

Yes, he knew that, Lily would never get him into trouble.

He opened the bag and slowly, one by one, drew out the small round paper-wrapped objects and, unwrapping one, he put it on his palm and held it out for her to see.

After staring at it she said to him, "Is it a bead?"

"No."

"What is it then?"

He thought for a moment. "It's a piece of glass, hard glass."

"Glass?"

"Aye."

Now lifting the stone from the paper and holding it between his finger and thumb, he extended his arm and opened his fingers. The gem made no impression when it hit the choppy surface. One second it was falling, and in a split second it was gone.

One after another he unwrapped the stones, and each time he looked at Lily before going through the process of dropping them into the water, until there was only one left ... the big stone, the bonny stone with the pinky-red lights in it.

Lily was staring at him. He could see the stone set in a brooch pinned to the front of her frock. He could see the money from the stone buying her a new dress; and not one, oh no. This kind of stone would, he knew, buy her dozens of new dresses. His voice thick, like that of a fully grown man, he said to her, "What'll you think of me in years to come if I can never earn more than ten shilling a week?"

Her answer came on a warm smile, "Same as I do now, Rory."

He held the stone for a moment longer, but he did not take it between his finger and thumb; instead he held out his arm, his palm upwards, and slowly tilting it he watched the ruby fall through the air and enter the water. Unlike the other stones, however, it seemed to rest for a second on the surface and its lights flashed a myriad farewell at him. Had he been a fool?

He turned his head and looked at Lily. Ten shillings a week for the rest of his life. That's all he'd ever be able to offer her, and she'd be hard pushed to make that spin out as the years went on. And he had just thrown a fortune into the river! Never again would such luck come his way.

"Feel better now, Rory?"

Slowly he smiled at her. He had just thought that never again would he be lucky; but he was lucky at this moment for he had Lily and she was different from all other lasses. He thought of that cheeky monkey who had tried to pull the bedclothes off him.

Then suddenly, in the middle of the Don bridge, and with an old man passing them, Lily leant forward and kissed him. Smack on the mouth she kissed him. He couldn't remember ever being kissed before, except by his ma when he was leaving home to go into the wheelwright's shop, and by their Edna and Mabel, and that once by Mrs Cornwallis. But this was different.

He gaped at Lily. Her face was pink. She looked bonny, really bonny. Her eyes were soft brown and her lips red. Fancy anybody calling her plain ...

When the old man laughed, Lily turned and, lifting up her skirts, ran off the bridge and along the road.

Rory stood for a moment watching her until the old man cried at him, "What you standin' there like a stook for, lad? Go on, man, an' put a stop to her gallop."

And on a laugh he leapt off the bridge and raced after her, to put a stop to her gallop; and when he reached her he caught her hand, but didn't stop running. Like this they ran until they reached the fells, and there, panting and laughing, they slowed down to a walk, their hands swinging between them, not speaking, just looking at each other every now and then.

And this is how they walked until they came in sight of the village. Then the magic slid away and he let go of her hand and, walking sedately, he said, "We'll have a fight on our hands against your da."

To this she answered, "I'm ready for it if you are, Rory."

He looked at her and said, "No one was ever more ready than me, Lily."

They had stopped and he just might have been bold enough to kiss her, but at that moment Sammy came dashing along the road towards them, crying, "Eeh! our Rory, where've you been? The missis 'as been calling for you everywhere."

"Something wrong?"

"No, no, I don't think so, only the cabs've gone an' most of the folk. But ... but Mr Morley Cornwallis and his missis and their Bernie are in the room sittin' waitin' for summit, and the missis won't let them get started afore you come, an' there's another man there."

"Not the man who was here yesterday?"

"Oh no. This one was at the funeral. He comes from Shields way, I think. He's the one 'twas here t'other day, after you went away. You know, I told you."

As Rory hurried down the village street with Lily on one side of him and Sammy trotting at the other, he literally wiped the happiness of the last hour from his face by passing his hand around it two or three times. He mustn't go in looking as if he were glad about something. 'Twasn't fitting. And he shouldn't feel glad about anything a day like this and the master not yet cold in his grave. Why were they waiting for him? He could have understood if he had been wanted in the shop, but it was closed the day, naturally.

At the foot of the stairs he said to Sammy, "You stay there." He didn't say that to Lily for she had a right to come up, her family apparently being already present.

He had his cap in his hand when he entered the room, and he felt his colour rising again when all eyes were turned on him. There, sitting round the table that was laden with foodstuffs, were Morley Cornwallis and his wife, and their Bernie, Mrs Beeney from the shop, old Peter Tollett, Benny Croft, the missis and the strange man.

"Come in, boy," said Mrs Cornwallis, "and take a seat." She pointed to the only vacant seat in the room, which was the master's chair standing by the fireplace. He walked up to it but hesitated to sit down, until she nodded at him, saying, "Be seated."

Lily was now standing behind her parents and her mother was saying to her, "Where do you think you've been?" and she gulped before she answered 'In . . . in the house, Ma. I . . . I went straight home."

The strange man, now tapping the tips of his fingers on the table, said in a thin, high voice, "Seeing that we're all here at last we can now proceed with the business, of which I'm sure you're all anxious to learn." He paused and swept the whole company with a fierce glance, directed over the top of his spectacles and from under bushy brows, before he finished, "Concerning the ins and outs of the deceased's wishes."

No one spoke, but everyone present with the exception of Mrs Cornwallis and Rory moved in their seats.

The man now drew from a long envelope a thick sheet of paper which was folded in half; then again surveying the company from over his glasses he began to read: "I, John William Cornwallis, have requested that the solicitor, Mr Francis Armitage, of Armitage, Rutland and Coles, come to me to take down my last statement.

"Although my back be broken, I am still of sound mind on this day, Tuesday, the twenty-eighth of October, eighteen hundred and fifty-one, and I wish him or his clerk to take down my words as I say them.

"Being in dire trouble I do not think I have long to live and want my wishes carried out as follows:-

"I leave to my wife, Rose Cornwallis, who has been a good wife and more to me, I leave to her the business of the wheelwright's shop and the debts owing to it, together with what is in the purse, which place she knows of. The sum in it at present stands at two hundred and fifty sovereigns and thirty-four half-sovereigns. I also leave to her in trust the sum that is held in the bank in Newcastle which amount is known to her and need not be mentioned.

"To her good friend, Emily Beeney, I leave the sum of ten pounds. This, and the next two amounts I will state, will come out of the shop profits and the money due to me from Sam Kirkup, which is twenty-four pounds for waggon as complete, and from Septimus Tyler nine pounds ten shillings for cart as complete, and from Emily Brace ten shillings for a poss stick, and eighty feet of soft pailing for pig sties at a penny a foot, which amounts to six shillings and eightpence. These articles on top of four other bills she has unpaid come to seven pounds fifteen. But I doubt if she will pay speedily though she is not short of money – may ask for debt to be paid off in pig meat.

"Now to Peter Tollett who has worked faithfully for me, and my father before me, I leave ten sovereigns and the promise that he will be paid the sum of five shillings a week when he retires, that is should he consent to stay

on in the shop for another three years, by which time the boy, Rodney McAlister, shall have completed his apprenticeship, and during that period instruct him in everything that will help him towards becoming a first-class craftsman in our trade. Should he not comply with my wish then his pension will stand as we arranged at two shillings a week.

"To Benny Croft I leave the sum of five pounds and the promise that should he, too, stay and help in the shop and not wander about as he does every year, he will, when his time comes, be given the same pension as stated above."

At this point the solicitor again surveyed the company over his spectacles. Taking a sip from his glass, which was half full of whisky, he straightened his shoulders, wrinkled his nose, then said, "Remember I am quoting the deceased's own words," and, turning the page of the folded paper, he now read: "I am come to the point very near to my heart. It concerns the boy, my apprentice, Rodney McAlister. To him I leave the sum of twenty pounds to do what he likes. It is in payment for a service he has rendered me, and I say to him, now that I am no longer here I have, since shortly after he came into my employ, looked upon him as a son, as has my wife, and had it not been that he was firmly established with his own family we would have taken him legally as our son. Both my wife and myself are of the opinion that he has a regard for us, so, therefore, I am saying to him this. If he will promise when his time is up to stay with the shop and take its concerns on his shoulders and, as much as lies within his power, look after my wife as a son would and stay with her in this house, I propose to do towards him as follows ... on the death of my wife he is to have the house and business of the wheelwright's shop and the freehold land on which it stands, together with the cottage which I promised him for his people, and which they can remain in as long as he stays in my wife's service. Should he be taken away by death, his family are free to stay in the cottage until such time as both father and mother are dead.

"Further, at my wife's death I leave the monies in the Newcastle Bank in his trust, and bid him use the interest only every year to help three poor families in that they eat and be housed well. Although he could have access to the capital I ask him not to use this unless in dire need. By the time he hears my words read he will understand why I make this request.

"I have no more to say except perhaps to remind you, boy, of my words when we last parted. There is nobody in the world all black and nobody all white. Look after my wife and be a son to her. God bless you both.

Signed this day, Tuesday, the twenty-eighth of October, eighteen hundred and fifty-one.

Witnessed by Septimus George Roberts, Physician, and Michael Westbury, Clerk."

The solicitor now took his spectacles off and wiped them. He did not cast a glance around the table as he did so, but kept it fixed on the polishing of the lens. Not until he had cleaned them to his satisfaction did he replace them. Then he looked at Rory, as everyone else in the room was doing, and Rory, sitting well back in the chair now, for he needed support, gaped at them.

He couldn't believe it. He hadn't been able to believe his ears for the last three or four minutes. His eyes met those of the missis; her glance was soft and tear-filled. He wanted to get up, go to her and say, "I would have looked after you as best I could without anything." But he couldn't for, as he put it to himself, he was all tosticated.

His gaze was snapped away from Mrs Cornwallis's by a long drawn out snort of indignation, and not one, but two. Both Morley Cornwallis and his wife were on their feet and Morley, walking up by the side of the table, gripped the back of each chair in his passage until he stood in front of Rory, and through gritted teeth said, "You've wormed your way in all right, boy, haven't you?

But it's not goin' to work."

"Who are you to say what's goin' to work and what isn't?" Mrs Cornwallis was on her feet now. "I'll thank you, Morley, to see to your own affairs."

"Rosie!" Morley Cornwallis was wagging his finger at her. "Now 'tisn't fair. John and me were kin, and we too are kin." He pointed at her. "And he never mentioned me."

"We're not kin, Morley, not that it matters. An' you were only second cousin to him, and not even that if it was worked out properly. You've no claim whatever on him, never had."

"We've more claim than him." It was Mary Ann Cornwallis now putting her spoke in as she thrust out her arm towards Rory.

Mrs Cornwallis, now facing the enraged woman, said quietly, "Think back. What have you ever done for us, Mary Ann, now what? The only thing you've done is give advice, an' not good advice either. And you, Morley, have never put a pennorth of business our way. You've diverted it to Jarrow or Primrose and as far away as Felling rather than let John have it. Oh, we've known ... Well now, as the saying goes, as you sow so shall ye reap. This boy here's done more for John in a few days than both of you in a lifetime. There's John's will." She pointed now to the paper that the solicitor was folding up and putting back into the envelope. "It's legal, it stays. And the boy stays."

Mrs Cornwallis now turned and looked at Rory who had risen to his feet and taken a step towards her, but at this particular moment, if his life had depended on it, he could not have uttered a word. As he said afterwards, he was too flabbergasted.

He stood now beside Rosie Cornwallis watching the company depart, speaking their condolences but their minds not really on it. Even Peter Tollett and Benny Croft looked amazed.

The Morley Cornwallises were the last to leave, still

seething but seeming reluctant to go. Eventually, Morley, pushing his wife and Lily out of the door and saying to his son, "Come on Bernie, out of this," went to follow them, but stopped and, turning slowly, looked at Mrs Cornwallis and said, "This money in the Newcastle Bank, where did he get it? Must be a tidy sum to get interest like that. How did he come by it? I've never known him to have anything but what he got from the shop?"

"It would appear, Morley, that you didn't know everything. How he came by it is his business, and he's gone now, more's the pity. You can't ask him, an' I'll never tell you, so it's no use ferretin'. Good-day to you, Morley ... And thanks for coming to help lay him by."

Rory watched the man's chest swell to almost twice its size with indignation, and when the door banged he thought, "Eeh! that's disrespectful on a day like this."

Left alone with Mrs Cornwallis, he looked at her shyly, and she said, "Well, boy!"

"I ... I don't know what to say, Missis; I'm ... I'm staggered."

"I only want to hear you say one thing, boy, that you're pleased with the arrangements your master made."

"Oh aye, Missis, oh aye. I'll never be able to pay you back in gratitude, or owt else."

"You'll pay me back, boy. In fact, you've been paying in advance for years, and I thank God I've got you this night. Go downstairs now and bring up Sammy, he'll help to finish off some of this food, and what's over you'll take to the cottage for your people's comin' the morrow. They're movin' the morrow, aren't they?"

"Yes, Missis."

"By the way, Rory." She turned to the fire and pushed the kettle along the hob. "What do you call your mother, Mother or Mam or Ma?"

"Ma."

"Well, do you think you could call me Mam instead of Missis?"

165

In the moment that he paused before answering he thought it was strange, people's needs, they were all different. "Aye . . . Mam," he said hesitantly; then turned round quickly and went out of the room and down the stairs and called to Sammy.

Sammy came out of the wheelwright's shop itself. He looked slightly frightened. "The blacksmith," he said, "he looked real mad, real mad."

"Don't you worry about him, you needn't worry about nothing, Sammy, not for a long time, I'm set, we're all set. Remember, the morrow they're all comin' to the cottage. Come up now and eat your supper."

Sammy went ahead of him up the stairs but before he reached the top he turned and said solemnly, "It's hard to take in, isn't it, Rory?"

And Rory, rubbing the boy's head gently, said, "Aye, young 'un, it's hard to take in."

When they entered the room Mrs Cornwallis said, "Come and sit up, both of you, and have your fill."

And after they'd both eaten and helped to clear the table and brought upstairs the coal and the water and the wood, she looked at Rory, and said, "Other nights ahead we'll sit by the fire for a while an' maybe read a bit, but tonight I'm goin' straight to my bed, for I'm sad at heart and very tired. You understand, boy?"

"Aye, Mam, I do," he said.

"But one thing more I'll say to you afore I go, boy, an' it's just this. You'll have to be wary of Morley Cornwallis. I've been saying to meself he can't do anything, 'cos I can't see what he can do, but knowin' him I fear he'll get up to something, so be on your guard, boy."

"I will, I will, Missis . . . Mam."

"Good-night, boy." She bent forward and kissed him on the cheek; then stooping, she did the same to Sammy, and as she turned away she said, "I'll leave you to lock up the doors. Better start the way we mean to go on." And again he said, "Yes, Mam."

Chapter Nine

The very next morning about noon, when Rory walked out of the village and on to the fells it was made clear to him what Morley Cornwallis was up to.

Rory had had a busy morning. He had risen at five, got the fires going, opened the shop, and had the stove alight before Peter Tollett and Benny Croft arrived. And when they did arrive they had looked hard at him, wondering no doubt what attitude he would now adopt towards them. But he had stood before them and said, "Nothin's changed, I'm still an apprentice, an' you both could buy an' sell me in the trade. I've got to depend on you now to learn me."

They had answered almost in one breath. "We're for you, boy," and Peter Tollett had put his hand on his shoulder, saying, "What I know, you'll know afore I'm finished, an' if you haven't taken it on in three years then I'll stay till you do. What do you say to that?"

"You couldn't be fairer, Peter."

And when Benny Croft, on a merry laugh, said, "And me jauntin' days are over. I'll help you all I can, me word on it."

"Thank you, Benny. Thank you both."

He had worked hard until half-past eleven. Then,

having washed himself under the pump, he went upstairs and changed into an old, but clean coat and trousers. But on the sight of him Mrs Cornwallis exclaimed, "Oh! boy, you must get a better garb than that. Make it your business come Saturday to go into Shields."

He had smiled widely at her as he replied, "Aye, Mam."

"An' you must wear a collar in future." Her fingers tentatively touched the top button of his shirt, and again he smiled and said, "Aye, Mam."

"Well, don't dawdle. Get yourself away, or you'll find they'll be moved afore you get there."

"Yes, Mam. Good-bye." He paused at the door and exchanged a smile with her, and she said "Good-bye, boy. But here, wait." She lifted the sack of food from the table. "Look what you're forgettin', you'd forget your head if it was loose."

He laughed widely now. "I would, I would an' all. Good-bye again."

"Good-bye, boy," she answered, and he went down the stairs at a run.

Different people in the village street had nodded at him but hadn't spoken, and he knew that they were still viewing him with surprise.

He passed the blacksmith's open door, and there was Bernie Cornwallis standing near the anvil. He was surprised that he didn't come to the door and spit abuse at him. Feeling somewhat cocky, he slowed his step to give him a chance, in case he couldn't leave the anvil for the moment, but Bernie made no move.

Well! well! the things you learned on a bright, windy day. He felt happy, uplifted, yet he knew he shouldn't feel like this when only yesterday the master had been buried. But somehow he knew this was the way the master would want him to be, bright, uplifted, looking forward; and Ben would too. Aye, Ben would too. He had dreamed of Ben last night.

He had just turned the bend in the road and was walking by the stone wall that bordered the farm when he heard quick footsteps behind.

"Rory! Rory!"

When Lily came hurrying round the bend, a milk can in her hand, his eyes widened for she was dressed as he had never seen her before. She slowed her step before she reached him and when she stopped he looked her up and down. Her face was bright and showing a happiness that denied she could ever be plain. His own face stretched when she lifted the bottom of her dress upwards and dropped a curtsey.

He watched her run to the wall and place the can on top of it, as she had done some days previously. But this time she laid her head on her folded arms and began to laugh uncontrollably.

He stood over her, laughing too, but without any idea of what he was laughing about. "What's up with you? What's happened you?" he asked her.

She lifted her head. Her face wet with tears from laughing so much, she said, "Don't you see? I've got me new frock on."

"Aye," he said, still puzzled. "I'm not blind, an' . . . an' it suits you, you look bonny." Then his manner and face sobering, he asked, "Is it 'cos Frank Jackson's expected?"

She shook her head and he said, "No?" and she repeated, "No."

"What for then?"

"For you!" Her voice wasn't shy, and somehow he thought it should have been when she was making such a statement, until she added in a voice that was a good imitation of her father's. "'Put your new frock on, girl, and go down and see your Aunt Rosie. It's lonely she'll be the day.' And as I put it on I thought, me new frock's not goin' to help me Aunt Rosie any, an' I couldn't understand it until I heard our Bernie call to me ma in a loud whisper, 'He's just gone past makin' for the fells,' and then . . ." At this point Lily bowed her head and put

169

her hand over her mouth and started to laugh again, and Rory said, "And then ... Well! go on, tell us."

Her eyes bright and blinking, she now said, "Me ma came in like a divil in a gale of wind, thrust the milk can into me hand and almost pushed me out, saying, 'Go an' get a quart.' And when I asked her what she wanted a second quart for 'cos I'd already been once, she said, 'I'm goin' to make a puddin'. And don't you dawdle on the road talkin' to Rory McAlister,' she said, 'mind I'm tellin' you.'"

They were silent now, staring at each other.

"Do you see, Rory?"

"See what?"

"O – oh!" she screwed up her eyes tight and pushed him with the flat of her hand. "They've decided that you're a better catch now than Frank Jackson, and I'm to cock me cap at you."

"No!"

"Aye, isn't it funny?"

"Aw, Lily." He now leant against the wall and, his shoulders shaking, he said, "Aye, it is funny."

"You know, I couldn't get out quick enough, I nearly burst. Mind –" she nodded her head at him – "you won't have to make things easy for me; you'll take no notice of me when they're about. I want to see them breakin' their necks to push me at you, an' the more you keep cool the more cans of milk I'll be sent for." She bowed her head now and giggled as she added, "And the more times I'll be sent down to comfort me Aunt Rosie." Then, her face becoming serious for a moment, she ended, "It's lucky me Aunt Rosie likes me."

"Aye, 'tis. That makes the two of us."

They became quiet, staring again at each other. Then of a sudden he said, "I've got to be goin', I'm movin' me folks into the cottage." But he didn't turn away from her, nor she from him ... Swiftly now he bent forward and put his lips on hers; and as swiftly he turned about and left her.

When he had gone about a dozen steps he looked over his shoulder. She was still standing where he had left her. "Ta-ra, Rory," she cried. He stopped for a moment. "Ta-ra, Lily," he answered. Then he jerked his head and winked at her; and at this she let out a high laugh, picked up the can, sat on top of the wall and swung her legs over, then ran across the field.

His head in the air, his shoulders squared as befitted a man with responsibilities, Rory walked on. And he wasn't unaware of the responsibilities that he had taken on. For years now he had had to look after his family, but now he had a second home, and in a way another mother to care for; on top of which the prosperity of the wheelwright's business would be on his shoulders. And if this wasn't enough, his mind was already planning a fourth responsibility, and he was old enough to know what that led to, another home and children. But he asked himself aloud what they all amounted to after all, for anybody who had served his time, be it only two days, in the dangerous craft of transporting blue baccy was prepared for anything.

Moreover, he considered that it had taken a man to hold a fortune in his hand and drop it piece by piece into the river. He was no longer a lad, or a boy. Come Saturday he was going in to the Bank in Newcastle, and afterwards he was going to a real tailor's to get himself a new suit.

From now on he was a man, Mr Rory McAlister.